THE CULL OF LIONS

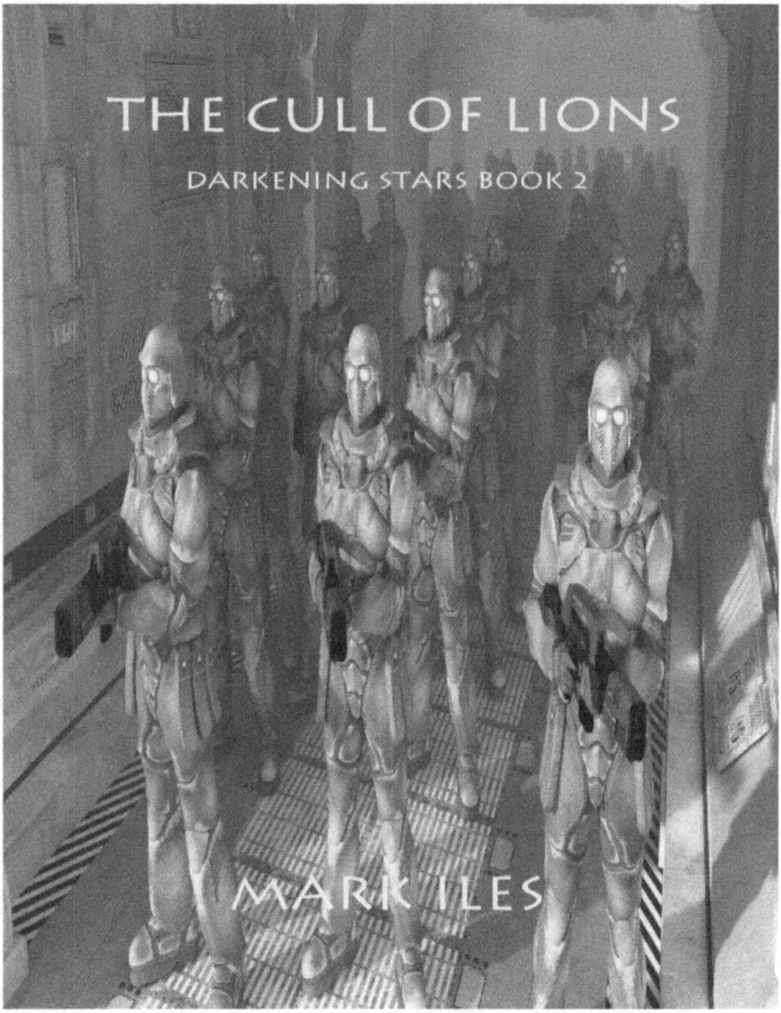

DARKENING STARS BOOK 2

MARK ILES

THE CULL OF LIONS

The Darkening Stars Book II

By

Mark Iles

Cover Art:
MLCdesigns4You

Publisher's Note:

This is a work of fiction. All names, characters, places, and
events are the work of the author's imagination.

Any resemblance to real persons, places, or events is
coincidental.

Solstice Publishing - www.solsticepublishing.com

Copyright 2014

Mark Iles

Dedication

To the Communications Branch and shipmates of HMS Invincible, all members of the British Task Force of 1982 and to the Falkland Islanders; but a special mention to those who remained behind, forever on patrol.

Prologue

As a young child, Selena Dillon's world is torn apart when her parents are forced to divorce by the planets ruler. The Queen then forces Selena's father to marry her, but shortly after he dies in suspicious circumstances which fuels the belief that he was murdered for refusing the Queen's demands. Overcome with grief Selena's mother commits suicide in front of her and sets in motion a stream of events that will change the fate of humanity.

As an adult Selena joins a band of freedom fighters, determined to rid the world of the Queen. When she and her comrades are caught trying to kill her they're tried and found guilty for the murder of the guards and the attempted murder of the sovereign. Given the choice of either the death penalty or twenty–five years' service in the penal regiments Selena chooses the latter, knowing that if she can survive then one day she'll be able to come back and try again.

Much to her surprise Selena excels at basic training and, following an incident where she turns the tables on her instructors she meets Commodore Van Pluy, who selects her for officer training. Passing selection with ease Selena is then promoted and posted to a small group of vessels on anti-piracy patrol, along with Kes Phillips — her friend from basic training who serves as her sergeant. Her brutal reprisals against the pirates for their harsh treatment of their captives, earns her a fearful reputation.

When her suspicions are raised at the pirates' successes, and their ease at evading Selena's ships, she soon discovers a mole who had been tipping the criminals off. Planting information with the pirates that their spy has been discovered and betrayed them in turn for her freedom, Selena leaves the unfortunate woman planet-side to be murdered. Selena then tracks down the pirate horde, capturing them and their government cohorts.

But something else is happening in the far reaches of the galaxy, rumours say that the outer colonies are falling silent and it's soon discovered that they're being attacked by the alien Manta, a race hell bent on mankind's destruction. Selena and Kes are called to a meeting by Commodore Van Pluy, where he informs them that unless something can be done about the Manta, and soon, then mankind is doomed. Humanity's weapons are ineffective against the alien ships and the military have had to resort to a scorched-Earth policy, destroying any human world captured by the enemy. With the Federation of Man's Fleet almost destroyed, and their colonies being overrun, the human race is facing annihilation.

Van Pluy's plan is simple. He gives Selena command of the *Dutch Lady,* a ship filled with planet busters and a one-way mission, to attack and destroy the aliens' home world. But little does Selena know that she'll fall in love with her pilot, that there's a serial killer in her crew who's responsible for the death of another crew member's wife, and that this man is determined to get his revenge — no matter what the cost.

During a skirmish with the enemy the *Magellan,* their transport to the *Dutch Lady,* is damaged and they're forced to land on Loreen, a planet of apparent little consequence. After helping to defend the military base from a joint force of rebels and colonists determined to seize the *Magellan* and make their escape, Selena calms the colonists with promises of food and aid they desperately need, then sets them free despite their crime of helping the rebels. The grateful colonists then reveal the existence of a strange building hidden within a hill. Investigating it they discover a maze of interlocking underground tunnels that lead to other worlds. These worlds were once inhabited by the mythical ForeRunners, a race of ancient humans who were defeated by the alien Manta in a long forgotten war.

Realising the importance of the discovery Selena promises the colonists her utmost protection from the alien invaders, in return for citizenship for every penal soldier, past, present and future. With the agreement signed Selena and her crew continue on their way in the *Magellan* and soon board their asteroid vessel.

As they launch their attack on the enemy planet the *Dutch Lady* battles its way through clouds of fighters and battle stations while the Manta break through the surface of their asteroid ship. Just before impact Selena and the others escape in a lifeboat, only to be hit by enemy fire and crash land on a backwater world. With Bryn killed during the landing Selena finally comes to understand why her mother couldn't live without the man she so desperately loved. When the *Magellan* finally arrives to rescue the survivors Selena stays behind, planning to die at her lover's grave when the planet is destroyed. But at the last moment Selena is rescued by Kes and Singh, who tell her that Hope, the daughter of friends on the planet Loreen, is now missing and that they need to find her. They also tell Selena that the Manta were not destroyed in their attack, some of the enemy survived and have now invaded Selena's home world. Realising that she must ignore her feelings and honour her obligations Selena and the other survivors travel back to Loreen to help mankind once more.

Chapter One

"We're coming out of hyperspace now, Ma'am," Singh reported, turning his head to look back over his left shoulder towards Selena. "We're entering the Loreen system."

"How long before we get there?" Selena asked, finger combing her long blonde hair.

"Only a couple of hours, Ma'am." Singh scrunched his face up in puzzlement as he looked at the monitors. "Hang on, there's another ship out here. It's running silent but turning towards us."

"Is it one of ours?" she asked, her heart skipping a beat. "We don't want to get caught out here in a shuttle by the Manta."

"Looks like a Federation destroyer, but it's turned all transponders off and is accelerating. It doesn't make sense"

"Could it be a pirate?" Kes asked. "We did upset those guys some time back and no doubt there's a few still looking for revenge."

Selena looked at her swarthy sergeant, his closely cropped ginger hair starting to show more profusely. "It could be. Singh, accelerate to full speed, whatever's going on this doesn't feel right."

Singh complied and the little craft shot forward. "It's still closing. Their weapon systems have been activated."

"Faster Singh, get us out of here."

"We're at full speed already." Then he breathed a sigh of satisfaction. "They've turned away and Loreen's hailing us. Challenge-and-reply went well, and their automatic defences have stood down."

"Well, that's a relief. We'll ask what they know about that ship when we land. Is there any news from the planet?" Selena was anxious to hear about their missing friends Franks, Amanda and their daughter Hope. "Wow," she said, leaning forward for a better view out of the forward screen. "Just look at the size of those battle stations. It's hard to believe it's only four years since we were last here. How many of them are there?"

"There's ten around Loreen itself," Singh replied. "Apparently there are other bases being set up further out in the system and they also have battle stations defending them. It looks as though we're taking the defence of this system pretty seriously."

A slight noise made Selena turn around. Her eyes narrowed. "Hey why's that survival computer, Henry, with us? Are you planning on making more hooch, Singh?" She knew full well Singh used the machine's abilities to ferment fruit into alcohol. It had been one of the things that made their shipwrecking bearable.

"I'll have you know Arthur spent a long time working on Henry, before he was killed. That robot even knows how to play chess. The hooch has nothing to do with it, Ma'am, honestly…"

Selena eyed her slim Indian friend, a slight smile on her face. "Do you honestly expect me to believe that?"

He smirked. "Nope, but I'm pretty sure Henry will come in handy for something. It would have been such a waste to leave him behind."

Selena looked at the silver box-like contraption again, with its folded arms tucked in tightly to its sides. She studied her reflection in the gleaming metal for a moment, blue eyes and blonde hair, plump lips that thinned with distaste. "Singh, you really need to get a dog."

Kes snorted, as Singh guided their shuttle past the battle stations and the countless sleek black warships in orbit and then entered Loreen's atmosphere. Moments later they were winging their way over the gentle, undulating waves of the ocean towards the spaceport.

As their small ship slowed, hovered and finally landed Selena was surprised at how much the base had grown in such a short time. Spacecraft were landing and unloading in the spaceport now buried inside the expanded fortress, then being filled with what looked like local produce before taking off again with hardly a pause. It was all hustle and bustle. Around them scores of locals and robots could be seen swarming over structures and erecting buildings. The citadel had to have at least doubled in size since they were last here, and on one side you could see construction vehicles and piles of stores that showed that the walls were about to be moved out even further.

As they strode down the gangway they saw the slim figure of Lieutenant Kotes, from the *Magellan*, waiting for them.

"I'm glad you finally made it, Commander," he said, saluting as they stopped in front of him.

"I'm sorry if I worried you when I didn't evacuate, back on that world where we crashed," Selena returned his salute. "It was Singh and Kes who changed my mind about staying there. They told me Hope and her parents were missing and they needed my help. Is there any news?"

Kotes hadn't changed much, she mused. He was about five foot two with tight dark hair greying slightly just above his ears, and he was still at his demoted rank of Lieutenant despite their mission's success. Her report to the admiralty about him disobeying orders and attacking enemy ships, instead of ignoring them and taking her team directly to the *Dutch Lady*, had obviously played havoc with his career.

He held up a hand, as he led them across the tarmac, baking under the hot blue-tinged sun, forestalling further questions. "No, there's nothing new to tell you I'm afraid. We've an admiral in charge here now. He's had search parties out day and night looking for Hope and the others.

You know him apparently, a guy called Van Pluy. He asked me to take you directly to him the moment you landed."

"Van Pluy's an Admiral? That's fantastic news.' Selena replied, blue eyes twinkling. She stopped suddenly and held out her hand. To her delight Kotes shook it. "I know we've had our differences, Lieutenant," she said. "As far as I'm concerned that's in the past, let's move forward shall we?"

They had to speak loudly, their voices pausing or raising above the roar of ships taking off or landing. Behind it all was the babble of voices, as staff of all kinds worked on the ships and went about their errands.

"I've no problem with that at all, Commander, thank you. As you know, I was unaware of the importance of the *Dutch Lady's* mission, and what the repercussions my action could have had on mankind if we'd been lost. I still believe attacking those craft saved Bernard's Star and that I did the right thing at the time. For what it's worth, you still have my apologies."

Her grin put him at ease and, as he led the way to a skimmer, he continued to speak.

"Van Pluy was promoted and awarded medals galore after you destroyed the Manta's home world. One of the reasons he came here was to get away from all the fuss, says it was driving him mad. He's quite the celebrity now and hates it. He recently told a reporter if he didn't bugger off he'd have him shot on the spot, scared the poor fellow shitless. We all know what the press can be like, a pain in the ass at the best of times and the old man doesn't have a great deal of patience with them. He's coordinating the military build-up and the reinforcement of the system. Not many people knew about our presence here until recently, it was a bit of surprise to the regulars but I'll let Van Pluy tell you about that."

Selena looked up at the imposing battlements. With improved weapon systems and more buildings it was even more daunting than before. By the look of this place, and the sprawling constructions around it, this would soon lean towards being a city.

They boarded the skimmer and Kotes drove them carefully towards the main building, before setting down in the square in front of it. They noted in silence that a large rectangular plain-metal frame had been erected there, about which columns of the corps stood at ease.

"Punishment detail," Selena breathed. She hated this but understood the necessity for discipline.

When the craft had settled to the ground they all got out and joined the ranks of waiting troops, as protocol demanded. They stood at ease in one of the many platoons, feet apart and hands clasped behind their backs, facing the frame. They didn't have to wait long. A few moments later a young recruit was frogmarched out. He was stopped in front of the frame. His hands were attached by chains above him to either side, feet likewise to the bottom. His clothes were then cut away, leaving him completely naked in the sunlight and to the stares of his fellows. Then the punishment began.

A sergeant came up behind the offender, bull-whip in hand. Selena noticed Admiral Van Pluy and several senior officers watching silently from one side. Then an officer called them all to attention, their boots stamping together with a resounding crash, and he read out the charge of disobeying an order and stated the punishment of five lashes.

"You are reminded," the officer bellowed, "that had this been in a time of action this man would be executed right now."

A trooper began to count out loud. At each count the sergeant drew back his right hand, raising a thick brown leather-looking whip. As the loud crack reverberated around the square even the birds fell silent. The man sagged at the fifth strike, his back raw and bleeding, flesh ripped to the bone. That's when they stopped, unchained him and dismissed all those watching. Turning right, as one, they stamped their feet in a loud 'boom!' paused for a moment and began to amble off. Selena and the others watched the accused being carried to sick bay, their joy at returning to Loreen tempered somewhat by what they'd just witnessed.

Kotes turned away to a group of friends and remained chatting, while Selena and the others entered the main building and were shown into Van Pluy's office. The admiral, sitting behind his polished wooden desk, looked up as they entered. He took the large cigar out of his mouth, blew a cloud of fragrant bluish-grey smoke to one side then stood, shaking their hands and saying, "I'm glad to see you all, but bloody sad to hear about your losses. That must have been one hell of a fight back there. You did us proud, as I knew you would."

"Thank you, Sir. Congratulations on your promotion, by the way," Selena said, as she and the others sat down in the dark-red leather-like armchairs. She noted his now snowy hair and tired looks, the deep lines of his face and bags under his eyes. "We'd have been back a lot sooner but it appears someone forgot about us, despite the fact I understand our distress call was picked up. Tell me, Sir, why did you wait so long?"

"Straight to the heart of the matter as always, Selena." Van Pluy's face grew sombre as he brushed at the multi-coloured medal ribbons across the left breast of his uniform. "You weren't forgotten, if that's what you're thinking. Let's just say we needed you out of the way for a while. There were things going on that it was best you weren't involved in. You guys were heroes then and are now. We needed to keep you alive and somewhere safe. Things got pretty hairy here for a while."

"Somewhere safe?" Singh blurted. "The whole bloody planet was destroyed."

"You left us out there deliberately?" Selena asked coldly, shocked at the revelation despite herself and noting the way Singh tensed up beside her. She could feel anger starting to boil deep inside her, and her fists clenched tightly, the alloy fingernails digging into her palms.

"At ease, soldier." the admiral snapped, his eyes flashing, then he relaxed again and dragged once more on his cigar. "We didn't really have a choice. When people will see you now they'll remember what you achieved. It'll bring back their joy and take away some of the pain of the recent past. You'd have been no good to us dead. Let's just say you fly the flag of the penal regiments, you're a prime example of what we stand for. There are people out there who don't like that and would love for you to meet with an accident. We were looking out for you, so relax."

Van Pluy pressed a white button on his desk and moments later a steward appeared through a side door, carrying a tray laden with crystal tumblers, a bucket of ice and a large expensive-looking bottle of amber liquid. "That's genuine single malt, all the way from Scotland, on what's left of Earth," the admiral said. "I thought you deserved it. I know Singh appreciates a fine scotch. According to Lieutenant Kotes, Singh quite depleted his stock."

The twitch on Singh's lips spoke volumes.

Van Pluy poured them all a drink, added ice with a clink and sat on the edge of his desk. He raised his glass in a toast, took a sip and then set it down beside him on the dark-brown highly-polished wood. "Now, let's get back to our discussion. We didn't dare try to contact you, because any signals from yourselves could easily have given your location away.

"With Mantis destroyed things in the military changed considerably. Luckily I developed a feeling something wasn't right and alarm bells started ringing when the Admiralty became both elusive and reticent. I couldn't put my finger on exactly what the problem was, but it was my decision to keep your location secret, even from the President, and I'm glad I did. All everyone knew was that you'd completely disappeared after the battle. Only a limited number of my own personal staff had any idea what happened to you, and even fewer where you were. To be honest most people thought you were dead."

Van Pluy stood, picked up his glass and wandered over to the window, looking out at the lush green forest outside the town, stretching far into the distance. Taking a puff from his cigar, the ash dropped but dissolved in mid-air before it hit the floor. He put it into the transparent ashtray on his desk then cradled the crystal tumbler in both hands. He looked down at the softly clicking ice and said, "It appears the admiralty didn't relish the thought of thousands of battle-trained ex-convicts roaming their streets. They planned a rather nasty surprise for us, despite all we'd done and everything we'd achieved. We'd arranged for the second and third Penal Fleets to replenish at Bernard's Star and pick up much-needed supplies for Loreen. We had no reason to suspect anything out of the ordinary, but the bastards booby-trapped those stores with low-yield nukes and once our ships were on their way out of the system the bombs detonated.

"A large Regular Navy force then swept in and finished off the job. In a few moments those entire fleets ceased to exist. The regulars from the Federation of Man didn't offer a chance to surrender, and we lost an awful lot of our people that day. Luckily some of our ships were running behind schedule and they only arrived in the system as the battle was ending. A few of them managed to escape and bring us the bad news."

"My God, that explains the Federation destroyer that chased us as we came into the system," Selena said, sitting back in her chair. She was stunned. Taking a sip of the fiery golden liquid she swallowed and then sucked on a lump of ice, still unable to absorb the news of betrayal. "I'd heard there'd been losses but nothing about this at all. How many ships did we lose?"

"Eighty-seven in that one battle plus another fifteen or so over the next week, and that's without those that were badly damaged and in need of repairs. In all we've lost one hundred and two ships, not to mention the thousands of men and much needed supplies. The Federation of Man also hit some of our smaller bases at the same time, and their main fleet came out of hyperspace in the Loreen system three days after the tragedy and engaged us here. Lucky for us we had the battle stations up and running by that time. They weren't expecting that and we beat the living shit out of them. Both sides have been licking their wounds and growling at each other ever since. I'll get a patrol sent out to see if we can get rid of that destroyer. That kind of thing happens every now and again."

Van Pluy added another cube of ice to his drink. Then he swirled the liquid around, watching the ice dance about in the amber depths. The white hair and lines on his face showing the stress he'd been under.

"That was shortly after your attack on Mantis," Van Pluy continued. "When the news of what you did got out every person on every world cheered, and then this happened. Thank God we had Loreen to fall back to and had fortified her as quickly as we did. We even have shipyards in the inner system now, and thanks to them we're repairing our damaged ships and building others as quickly as we can."

Kes looked the Admiral straight in the eye. "Where does that leave us, Sir? We can't take on the whole FOM. They have hundreds of worlds, while all we have is Loreen and a few minor outposts and I guess if we're now the enemy then that means we won't be getting any reinforcements, either."

Van Pluy walked over to the blood-red wall on Selena's left. He clicked a switch on a dark screen. It instantly lit up to depict the layout of the Penal fleet by class of ship and number of vessels. Selena's eyebrows rose in surprise.

"It's not all doom and gloom," the admiral said "We made quite an impression on the outer colonies during the war. Many of them had been left high and dry by the Federation, when they withdrew their ships to protect their more important assets. Naturally those worlds felt quite aggrieved about being abandoned, and who can blame them? As soon as they heard about the FOM's treacherous attack at Bernard's Star they left them and joined us."

He turned to look out of the window and they followed his gaze, watching as the ships flitting back and forth in the space port beyond, as the admiral continued.

"Our combined fleets are more than a match for the regulars, if they try anything again. As part of our deal with the colonies we're upgrading their ships and battle stations to our latest specs. We've helped build space docks in some of their systems and we have contingents on many of their worlds, training their own armies. In return, all those serving in the Penal Regiments have received limited pardons from all allied worlds. In other words, while we still have to finish our sentences we can settle where we like when we finish our time: meanwhile we can continue to recruit directly from their Restorative Justice Programmes and even accept volunteers as well as criminals."

The admiral chuckled. "Why anyone would want to volunteer is beyond me, but believe me they do. So yes, luckily we're getting reinforcements again and lots of them too. Another bonus, of course, is that by having contingents on allied worlds we no longer have all of our eggs in one basket. All in all I'd say we've done remarkably well, considering."

~ 17 ~

"How about here on Loreen? It must have been quite a shock for the locals when the shit hit the fan." Selena observed.

"We've kept our word. These colonists need us and we need them. We bring in supplies, employ them, buy their goods and so far everyone's a winner. You did damn well here, Commander, when you got them to work with us, all of you did. I believe you're aware that the aliens survived the destruction of Mantis and their system; a colony ship of some kind got away. They've set up a base somewhere, although God knows where, and they've begun rebuilding their own forces too. But the worst news, as you know, is they've landed on Capulet."

"Yeah, we heard. I expect you know that's my home world. What's the situation there?"

Van Pluy picked up his cigar, stared at it for a moment before mashing it into the ashtray and selected another one from a wooden box on his desk. Then he returned to his chair, leant back and sucked on the cigar. It self-lit and as he puffed away and the aromatic smoke rose around him in purple clouds, which were instantly whipped away by the tiny air conditioner on his desk. He watched Selena carefully from behind hooded eyes. "Capulet's not lost…yet. Ironically both ourselves and the Federation have sent in reinforcements. Rather than us fighting each other we have a temporary truce while we try to save the planet. Luckily the Manta are nowhere near as powerful as they once were, thanks to you guys."

"So far we've managed to keep their ships away from the planet. We're bombing the hell out of their bases, not that we're getting through their shields, and are landing more troops all the time but there's been a high attrition rate. Thankfully we've abandoned the 'poisoned earth policy'. Personally I believe that saving the planet is do-able. I know where we stand with the Manta. It's the Federation I don't trust."

"I'd like to return to Capulet, Sir," Selena said, "to fight for it. Trouble is that's where I committed my crime and the rules state that I can't return there."

"Yes, I'm sure that you do want to go back, Commander. For your information those old rules don't apply anymore. The limited pardon means you can return to any allied world, even where you committed your crimes. But before you return home we need to find Hope, that's your priority at this moment in time. As the Colonist leaders here on Loreen, Franks and Amanda's support are vitally important to us and we need to keep them on board. Now, they've personally asked for your assistance and I'm not going to let them down. Once all this is resolved, then you can go to Capulet."

"Got it, and I'll do all I can. Is there anything else?"

"Yes, a couple of things. Lacey, you and Philips have both been awarded the Military Cross and promoted, which makes you, Lacey, a Lieutenant Commander and you, Philips, a Staff Sergeant." He paused to offer Selena a smile. "As for you, Dillon, you're one of the first to get the Sunburst; a new medal that's the highest award for bravery we have. You're also promoted to Captain with immediate effect," He handed her a small box, with her new buttons. "Congratulations and again, very well done."

Van Pluy added that the other members of the attack on Manta had been awarded the MC posthumously; and that a statue in honour of both ship's crews that had fought in the mission was to be erected in at one side of the citadels new parade ground.

Just then an alarm sounded, Van Pluy froze for a second and then he activated a wall screen. "What the hell's going on?" he demanded.

A harassed looking young female lieutenant looked back at the admiral. "Sir, intruders have broken into the labs."

"Intruders, Roberts? Explain."

~ 19 ~

"Aye, Sir, intruders. We've no idea where they came from but the area's being secured as we speak."

Van Pluy turned to Selena and the others. "You better come with me."

They arrived at the labs minutes later. Armed troops had already surrounded the building and a lieutenant with a face like a train crash was waiting for them. He came to attention crisply and saluted the admiral.

"Lieutenant, stay here and ensure no-one gets out," Van Pluy returned his salute. Then he gestured to several troops stood close by. "Corporal, you and those three men come with us."

The main door lay open and a burnt, electrical smell greeted them as they entered. Selena, Singh and Kes pulled their side-arms and followed as the four man team led the way, Van Pluy besides them. Much to their surprise the labs were empty. Then Selena glanced down and frowned.

"Christ, is that Henry?" she asked, prodding a mess on the floor with a booted foot.

"It was," Singh replied, staring in disbelief at the smouldering and badly melted heap of scrap. "What happened to him?"

"No idea," Kes interjected, his nose wrinkling at the acrid scent of burnt metal. "I fear your days as a brewer are numbered, shipmate."

Just then there was a faint noise from one of the many chests of equipment. Neon-blue lights flicked on and then ran up and down its sides. The sealed doors across the top began to sluggishly open upwards with a barely audible hum. A sickly, dull orange light spilled out and the troops' training kicked in. Selena and the others instantly took what cover they could, levelling their weapons at the strange sight that was slowly being revealed. As the doors opened more fully, and then recessed into the sides of the chest, a startlingly white man-shaped robot was lying on a bare metal trolley of sorts, straps across its shins and chest. The machine stirred slightly, rolling its shoulders and moving its head from side to side as it shuffled around on the trolley. Then, with a sudden snapping sound, the tan-coloured fabric restraints binding it to its silver bed fell away.

"What on Earth?" Singh gasped.

"Hold your fire," Van Pluy ordered, as the robot lay still again.

For a moment nothing happened and they all held their breaths, weapons at the ready. Then the robot opened electric-blue eyes and the head turned to look at them. Its hands reached up for the sides of the cabinet and the automaton pulled itself into a sitting position, before rubbing at its face with both hands. This caused a tooth-jarring scratching noise, like metal on metal, and at the eerie sound a low groan escaped it. To their disbelief the face flowed like liquid and rearranged itself into once familiar features. Then a voice they knew so well said, "Hello again, Commander. It's me, Arthur."

Chapter Two

"What the hell…Arthur?" Selena gasped. "It can't be, we buried you back on that God forsaken planet we just escaped from."

"Yeah, well, these are strange times. You never know what's going to happen next."

The robot's fingers again ran over its face, fluttering in a mannerism they all knew so well.

"How…" she lapsed into silence, before adding, "You're a robot."

"This has something to do with Henry, doesn't it?" Kes interrupted. "I saw you working on him every spare moment you had before we attacked Mantis. I guess you knew Singh would be tempted to keep hold of Henry, what with his interest in booze and Henry's built in survival encyclopaedias. I suppose it was also obvious that at some stage we'd come back here."

"I need you," Selena said turning to the tall, barrel-chested corporal. "What's your name?

"Braxis Ma'am," the man replied, looking a little daunted.

She raised an eyebrow. "What kind of a name is that?"

"The only one I have. You should hear what they called my brother."

"Arthur, are you for real?" Singh interrupted, staring at the robot as it climbed out of the coffin-shaped machine and stood backlit by the strange orange glow

"I'm as real as it gets. Hey, Braxis is it? Will you pass me something to put on? I may be a machine now but I still have a sense of decorum. There's a coverall over there on the stool next to you, be a good egg and pass it to me."

The corporal reached down, picked up the dark blue garment and tossed it one-handed, not once taking his eyes off the bizarre looking machine. Arthur's neon eyes looked somehow demonic. They watched him dress in silence and when Arthur had finished he looked at them. "You can put the guns down, I don't bite."

"Well, let's just say you've some explaining to do," Selena replied, keeping her side-arm raised. "Corporal Braxis, I want you and those other three men to take over from the lieutenant outside. Tell them the area is secured and it was only a false alarm. Then leave the other three men on guard outside and come back in alone. Whatever you do, don't let anyone enter this building. With your permission, Admiral?"

"Of course. Corporal Braxis, follow the Captain's orders. You will report directly to her from now on."

"Aye, Sir."

Braxis and the other three left immediately, shutting the outer doors noisily behind them. Selena and the others heard a muffled conversation, and then shouted commands from the lieutenant to fall out. A few moments later Braxis returned and stood behind them, weapon at the ready.

"So," Selena began, glancing at the remains of Henry while nudging them with her foot. "Was there something you didn't want us to know, Arthur?"

The white, ceramic-like lips twisted into a smirk. "Hardly, that wasn't exactly intentional. Before you ask, I've been working on this...mechanical body, for a long time. Call it what you will, clinical immortality if you like. That would make sense, because I've learned to copy a human being's consciousness and to download it into these shells. All you really need to do is to have the robot ready, and the means to transport and transfer the saved memory data."

"We don't have technology like that yet," Van Pluy said, chewing the limp end of a thick, dark and unlit cigar. "Neither the machines themselves or that transference crap you're on about. I've never even heard of it before."

~ 23 ~

"What you mean is we didn't have it yet but, like I said, I've been working on this for several years, in my own time of course. The trouble is a lot of my work has been destroyed." He nodded towards the remains of Henry.

"Bit of a coincidence, wouldn't you say?" Selena asked, deadpan.

Arthur looked at her silently, then blinked those sapphire eyes and changed the subject. "Where are the other members of the crew? What happened after we attacked?"

"You, Samantha, Bryn and Za'an were killed. As I said, we buried you after we crashed."

"Samantha?"

"You heard me, but for what it's worth I'm sorry. I know you two were close."

"Not as close as I'd like us to have been. That scum Za'an's gone too, eh?"

"As dead as the proverbial dodo," Singh replied, watching him closely.

"Good, then that saves me the effort of killing the bastard doesn't it."

"Actually, this raises quite an issue," the Admiral said. "The reports state that it was you who killed Za'an. You shot him in the head just before the lifeboat went down. In my eyes that makes you very much a murderer, Lieutenant."

"Ah, Admiral," Arthur replied. "That wasn't me at all. You see, this body wasn't around then. It's just a copy, as I mentioned. It was the other Arthur who killed Za'an. You can't blame me for a murder I didn't personally commit, now can you.

"My consciousness was uploaded into Henry just before the battle began. You brought Henry to Loreen and I was downloaded from him into this body you see before you. Consequently I only have the memories prior to the battle and know nothing of, nor am I responsible for,

~ 24 ~

Za'an's death. For the record, if he were alive now I'd kill that son of a bitch in a second. If possible I'd keep recreating and killing him for eternity. I have the memories of what he did to my wife, Mira, things like that are hard to deal with."

"Let's continue this in my office," Van Pluy said. "This lab isn't exactly the ideal place for discussions like this. Lieutenant Jones, for the time being, consider yourself under arrest. Braxis, I want all of this equipment secured. Allow no one near it."

*****

"The only way to describe it is to imagine the whole process is like a camera snapshot," Arthur said, reclining in one of the chairs in the Admiral's office. "You can only record your experiences and knowledge up to the specific moment of the upload, although of course you can update it later on. Everything that happens after that is lost forever. You also need to understand the old Arthur died and I'm a completely fresh one, but Arthur I am. Naturally because I am a new being I can only be responsible for things that have happened since my rebirth, certainly not before." He glanced at his three old companions and raised a questioning ceramic eyebrow. "Hey," he noted, "you've all been promoted."

"And awarded medals," Singh replied.

Arthur looked toward the Admiral. "Does that make me a Lieutenant Commander then, Sir?"

Van Pluy looked straight back at him. "You were promoted to that rank, yes, and also awarded the Military Cross."

Arthur's ceramic face gave an unnerving grin. "Brilliant, thanks!"

"But that was the old Arthur," Van Pluy replied dryly, "which means you're still a lieutenant." Ignoring the sapphire stare, the Admiral continued. "So how come we knew nothing of this technology? It's not just the

~ 25 ~

personality download, storage and transfer of the programme that enables it but also the robotic body you're in. The fact your face can make expressions is…well, bizarre to be honest. Oh, and incidentally, you do know anything you create while serving in the military belongs to the service, right? Yes, I want that research, Lieutenant, and I want it now."

Arthur tapped his head. "Some of it is up here, Sir, but I need to rebuild the equipment I had and figure out a lot of it again, particularly what went wrong, and then make a few tweaks. I stored all the data on Henry and he was destroyed, remember? I can recreate it of course, but it will take quite a while. Oh, and Singh," he turned to his colleague, "as I recall, you owe me a month's wages."

Singh's gaze flickered towards Selena, who raised her eyebrows at him.

"Ah, yeah, I'd forgotten about that. This doesn't prove anything at all, you cheated." Singh replied. "Besides, as the admiral says, that was the old Arthur." He looked at Selena and gave a nonchalant shrug. "I know you don't like gambling, Ma'am but, believe it or not, we had a bet as to whether there was life after death. That was after a few of those cocktails my ancestor invented. The long and the short of it is Arthur bet me a month's wages he would be able to prove there's life after death, by coming back from it himself. As far as I'm concerned this is cheating."

"Singh's right, this isn't proof of life after death," Kes interjected, "apart from the fact your personality hasn't improved much, you did cheat."

"Besides," Singh added, "what would you need money for? You're a robot."

"Upgrades, repairs, new bodies..."

"Am I the only one who thinks this is weird?" Kes muttered under his breath.

Arthur looked from the Admiral to Selena and back again. "Could someone tell me what happened during the battle?"

"After the attack on Mantis we escaped in the lifeboat," Selena replied. "Just as we hit hyperspace we took a couple of direct hits aft and started to lose power. We'd just channelled everything we had left to the engines to get us the hell out of there when a final shot slipped through the shields. There was an explosion and Samantha was killed. Singh and Bryn managed to set us down on a nearby planet but I was knocked out. When I woke I saw you lying next to Samantha. There was a gun in your hand and a bullet hole in Za'an's forehead, so it looks like you got your revenge after all. We buried the four of you next to a large pond in the forest where we crashed. You'd have liked it. It was a lovely spot and very peaceful, but it's all gone now. The planet was destroyed by meteorites and the shockwaves from the destruction of the Mantis system, shortly after we left."

Arthur was silent for a moment. Then he said, "I'm sorry to hear about the others, but obviously I'm not about Za'an. That bastard got off lightly."

"Moving on, how do we know you are who you say you are?" Van Pluy asked. "Apart from your bet with Singh, of course. A little more evidence would help."

Arthur turned to the Admiral. "Does Project Juliette ring any bells? It was the code name for my work on the deflector screens that's hopefully has since been adapted for the battle stations. I initially used the technology during the rebel attack on Loreen."

Van Pluy nodded steadily. "Okay, but how you achieved all of this is beyond me. So, you remember nothing at all about the attack on Mantis?"

"I rarely sleep, Sir, and had to find something to occupy my mind. With regard to your last question, I don't remember a thing. The only memories I have are up until the moment before we began our attack."

Selena, the admiral and the others all fired questions at Arthur, until they were finally in no doubt he was indeed who he claimed to be. As the questions trailed off, the admiral said, "Okay, we're going to run with this. Arthur, you're back in Captain Dillon's team, at least for the time being. We have an urgent job on and she's going to need your expertise but I'm going to need you back here once things settle down, working on those robotic bodies and other research in a fully staffed and secure lab. In the meantime, Franks's and Amanda's daughter is missing. She's somewhere down those damn tunnels and we have to find her. Do you any ideas where she might be?"

His eyes like twin plasma torches, Arthur replied, "Actually, Sir, yes I do. I guess it's time to go down the proverbial rabbit hole and back to Eden."

*****

"If Arthur can rediscover that knowledge," the Admiral said quietly to Selena, as they stood in the skimmer looking out at the lush, green forests slipping past below them, "can you imagine the benefits to both medicine and the military? Death would no longer be an issue, and when our troops are killed we could remake them into robot armies. Of course there's still the issue of Za'an's murder. I'm obviously not happy about it but we need to move on."

"While we're on the subject," Selena turned to face the admiral more fully. "Za'an was a murderous scumbag and he deserved to die. For your information I gave Arthur permission to kill him, but only when we'd completed the mission and gotten out of it in one piece. For what it's worth I don't regret giving him permission, or the fact he carried it out, one bit. Za'an was a complete psychopath, who cut up his victims then kept their body parts which he ate at his leisure. Arthur gave me his word he'd wait and he stuck to our deal, he always does. I have no problem at all with what he did."

"Why is it I get the feeling that if Arthur hadn't killed Za'an then he would have met an accident somewhere anyway?" Van Pluy reached up and patted his left breast pocket, as if to pluck free a cigar from the packet he always kept there. Then he changed his mind, ran fingers over his greying eyebrows and spoke so that everyone could hear. "Okay, you're no longer under arrest, Jones. The matter is closed. We need to focus on the search for Hope and her parents."

Arthur turned his ghostly face towards the Admiral. "Thank you, Sir. I've finished the upgrades on the bees and they're up and running. They've already searched several sites of interest. The thing that concerns me is a few of them haven't returned. One can only assume there are some defences within the rabbit holes which are, for some reason, eradicating my little pets."

"Bees, as in honey?" Kes asked, scanning the passing foliage.

"Actually they're tiny bots that look like flying insects," Van Pluy replied. "Arthur here designed the initial ones years ago. Since then he's just added a few extra algorithms."

"Of course he has," Kes replied. "A regular miracle worker isn't he."

Ignoring him the admiral continued. "We hoped to use them to investigate Eden's worlds but, for the time being, it seems the ForeRunner's are intent on keeping their secrets. Selena, I want your team to go to the site where Franks's and co were last and take charge of the rescue mission. We've a family to find. In the meantime, Arthur, as I said before you retain the rank of Lieutenant. That means you get to follow orders. Is that understood?"

"Perfectly, Admiral," Arthur replied.

"We've arrived," Van Pluy ignored Arthur, as the craft finally slowed and settled on the grass.

Selena and the others shouldered their weapons and strode purposely down the slim, metal plank that slid from the side of the skimmer and looked up at the imposing forested hillside before them. The path up it wasn't as long as Selena remembered but they were still breathing a little heavily by the time they reached the cave's entrance. She was surprised at the lack of defences and turned to the admiral, but he cut in before a word could leave her lips.

"I know what you're thinking, if this site's so important why isn't it better defended? Think about it, if the enemy managed to invade, then whatever defences we had here wouldn't last long anyway. If anything they'd give the site away. By having nothing here at all, it makes this place harder to discover and so protects it."

"That makes sense," Selena replied, looking again at the ocean view visible over the tree tops. She was worried about Van Pluy. The realisation of how much he'd aged shocked her.

"You ready yet?" the admiral asked a few moments later, before bracing himself and striding into the dark cave that now loomed before them.

Following him, Selena and the others looked around and then pulled up short. The Silver-coloured wall blocking their progress hadn't been there the last time they were here: nor had the auto-guns on the walls that were whirring gently as they tracked their progress. The admiral pressed his hand against a plate in a hidden recess. His prints and DNA confirmed, he typed an access code one-handed into a keyboard that slide out of the wall, while it also scanned his retina. Finally a door appeared in front of them and slid aside to reveal the chamber they remembered so well.

"That wall's made of the same material as the ForeRunner barrier in here," Van Pluy said as they stepped through. "We finally managed to analyse and reproduce it.

It's tough stuff and can't be detected. Well, at least with anything we have, which makes it ideal for keeping this place secure and under wraps."

They walked through into the inner chamber, where even the Admiral's ID was checked by two stern-faced sergeants while even more auto-guns and several armed men kept them covered. Satisfied, one of the sergeants stepped back and saluted Van Pluy.

"Welcome back, Admiral."

"Thank you, Baines. If you will?"

The sergeant made a hand gesture to the men on the right side of the room. There had been a control pedestal there once and the pile of rocks in front of it was now replaced by a wooden, intricately carved frame, one that bore the Penal Regiment crest of a black flying eagle on a white background reaching for unknown prey surrounded by a dark-blue circle.

Selena looked to the grey-metal barrier in front of them. The memory of seeing it for the first time a few years previously, with Bryn and the others, brought a moment's heartache. She forced Bryn from her mind as, once again, a hole appeared in the barrier and it spiralled away. Although she remembered this all so well, the brilliantly lit passageway leading down into the depths of the hillside still gave her pause. It had a warm, welcoming and heart-stopping beauty that simply took one's breath away.

"I'll leave you here, Captain," the admiral stopped short. "I've got far too much to do back at the shack, as much as I'd love to come with you. I'll see you all when you return. Good luck. Find Hope and the others, and bring them back safely."

The admiral turned abruptly and walked away, leaving them to walk down the sloping, silky tunnel.

"This place freaks me out," Singh observed. "It's unnatural. There's doesn't appear to be a light source, yet we can see everything so clearly."

Four inches taller than Selena's five foot two inches, she had to look up at Singh as he spoke.

"Yeah," Kes agreed, "and the air's here's so fresh, which is remarkable considering it had been sealed for God knows how long before we opened it."

At the end of the tunnel lay another barrier, more guards and several pod-mounted auto-guns. With a glance at the coverall-clad Arthur the guards eyes widened. Then they checked their ID's and, satisfied, they opened the entrance and ushered them through.

Selena and the others exited through the bole of a huge tree and found themselves standing ankle-high in thick green grass, looking up at a clear blue sky and the vast overhead canopy of the tree behind them. One of the first things they noticed was the warm, gentle wind kissing their faces, bringing with it the vibrant scent of wild flowers. Fruit trees flourished about them, their leaves moving gently in the breeze. Blackberry bushes brimmed with fruit bursting with juices. Selena had a momentary vision of Bryn striding up to a tree and quickly picking an apple, sinking his teeth into it before she could object. The sudden memory bought another sad smile and again she shook it away.

Braxis came to a halt besides her. "Holy shit!" he gasped, staring in disbelief at the scenery.

"Been studying poetry, have we?" Singh asked the barrel-chested trooper.

"How can we walk down a tunnel and end up in a different world?" Braxis asked. "It doesn't make sense."

"There are a lot of things here that don't make sense," Selena replied, walking into the clearing towards the base camp, while checking her weapon.

Like the Citadel back on Loreen, the camp in front of them increased in size and now clearly housed several hundred people, yet the tent-city pitched in the forest clearing had an ordered look about it. Skimmers zipped back and forth between the thick tree trunks, carrying stores and scores of uniformed and plain-clothed people on myriad tasks. The sheer hustle and bustle of it all spoke of the enormous resources being committed and used here in an attempt to discover more about the ForeRunners and Eden itself.

A soldier clad in black combats approached them and saluted Selena. He looked older than the average trooper. "Captain Dillon?" he asked.

"That's right."

"Can you come with me please, Ma'am? I have transport waiting."

The man quickly led them to a skimmer and, once they were aboard, the craft rose swiftly to several hundred feet and then tilted, before swooping to one side and shooting forward. The small stubby craft accelerated rapidly, until the forest below became a blur. In no time at all it was slowing again and they stopped in mid-air, turned and settled on the ground between huge trees towering far overhead. Braxis's mouth fell open at the sight of the hundreds of tunnels coming out of those massive trunks.

"Ye Gods," he gasped. "You're not going to tell me each of those leads to another world? That's amazing…what are those things?" He pointed towards the hundreds of shiny, knee-high silver machines marching back and forth from the tunnels on six thin legs that bent without seeming to have joints. On their backs they wore woven-grass baskets, which were filled with fruit and a multitude of other produce when they went into the tunnels. When they came back out again they were empty.

"We call them the Caretakers," Singh replied. They're a sort of robot, collecting food and so forth, and then taking it down those tunnels to God knows where."

Their driver stayed in the skimmer while Selena stood with Singh, Arthur, and Braxis, watching the caretakers trundling back and forth.

"Wonder why they even have legs," Singh queried with a frown. "Surely they should have antigravs?"

"Think about their job," Arthur replied, turning his brilliant eyes to him. "They're foragers created by the ForeRunners so they've been around a long time. Those limbs help them climb, dig, pick fruit and so forth. Climbing trees and going along branches, in and out of holes would be difficult without them."

"They give me the creeps," Braxis declared with a shudder. "They're like shiny, knee-high spiders. I'm not even sure what colour they are, silver mostly I know but, is it me or do they seem to change colour somehow, depending on the light?"

They watched the Caretakers picking fruit and other edibles, tossing it all into the baskets on their backs. When these were full they turned and marched towards the rabbit holes, before disappearing within. Selena studied the larger tunnels. "Well, we've quite a choice so take your pick."

Arthur remained silent for a moment, before pointing towards a tunnel a short distance away. "There."

"Is there any specific reason for choosing that one?" Singh enquired, quizzically.

"Of course there is. In case you haven't noticed, it's the only one of the larger tunnels the Caretakers are going into empty handed. That makes it different, and I think we should start there. Kids notice stuff like that, makes them curious."

To their surprise they saw Arthur was right, the caretakers were going in empty handed.

"Okay, the decision's made. Check your weapons," Selena ordered, her eyes and hands running over the sleek machine gun cradled in her arms. Like Singh's it was loaded with tiny but powerful depleted uranium rounds, while underneath the barrel of the shotgun had a variety of ammo which could be selected by her thumb with the click of a switch. She loved the fact the grenades were only slightly larger than the machine gun rounds, which meant a large number of the explosives could be carried at any one time, making it an awesome weapon.

Kes still preferred his microwave laser, while Braxis lovingly stroked a slicer. The beam from that weapon spread in a V-shape, although it could be narrowed when needed. It was handy for taking out close formations of troops, although the further the wide beam spread the weaker it became. They also carried throwing grenades and twelve-inch self-sharpening knives. Of them all only Arthur remained unarmed, the admiral had told Selena that he wasn't to be allowed a weapon until he'd proven he could be trusted.

"Stay here, with the vehicle," Selena told their driver.

Disappointment flickered over the man's deeply lined face. The long thick scar running down his left cheek jumped as his jaw worked and lips twitched, as if he was chewing something unsavoury. "Are you sure, Ma'am? No one's been down any of the other tunnels before, and I'm right handy in a fight."

"I'm sure you are, Private. What's your name?"

"Jack Harding, Captain."

"Well, Private Jack Harding, I'm sure you know that one of the first rules of combat is to ensure your exit is covered, so stay here and keep your weapon to hand and your eyes open. We might need to leave in a hurry."

When Selena and the others gingerly entered the rabbit hole the Caretakers simply walked around them. It wasn't long before they came to another door, this one remaining open to allow the steady stream of Caretakers in and out.

Selena and the others stepped out into a new and unexplored world, pausing briefly to take in the view. A deep-red, dusty soil lay beneath their feet, host to a tough yellow grass, while before them lay a vast motionless ocean. The sky was lilac and it was difficult to determine where the sea ended and where the sky began, for it all seemed to blend together to create the most bizarre effect. It was as if the land they were standing on was floating in Mid-air. The tunnel-tree they'd exited from was impressively tall and spread out far overhead, the same as those found back on Eden, yet the other trees were entirely different. Those were slim, considerably smaller, and their wispy leaves a light-green transparent mesh. Every now and then one of those strange leaves snapped shut and retracted into the dark-red bark, dragging unwilling insects and creatures similar to lizards and birds with it. Singh Shuddered and cursed, causing Kes to turn and frown at him.

"What's up?"

"It's those trees. They're the colour of blood. There's something about this place, it sets my teeth on edge."

Selena looked at him for a moment. "Blood Trees, that's an apt name for them. Arthur. We're here, so what's next?"

"I'd imagine Franks and Amanda would have set up a base camp relatively close to the rabbit hole. If I'm right, and this is the tunnel they came down, then they should be around here somewhere. Incidentally, I double checked and I was right, until now the search has only been focused entirely on Eden. There was just too much ground for them to cover on that world alone. No one will have searched this place at all, as far as I'm aware apart from Franks and Amanda, hopefully."

"Just how do you know that?"

"Because I looked it up before we set off from Base Camp. I have an eidetic memory."

Selena turned to him. The eerie half smile flowing and twisting on his unearthly face sent a chill right through her. "How does your face do that?"

"I was reborn with it, remember? It's a living material, both a gift and a curse. Some people might admire the ability, others probably despise it."

Selena didn't answer. The picture of Za'an's ruined forehead and lifeless eyes were stamped firmly in her memory, so she knew exactly how much of a threat he could be.

Arthur glanced at her and then continued. "By the way, this place needs a name. What about Arcadia? It's an alternative name for Eden, and as we've come from one version of it to another it kind of makes sense."

"Yes it does," she agreed. "Arcadia it is then."

"Ma'am?"

"What is it, Braxis?"

"Look, over there at the edge of the trees. There's a tent."

"Yea Gods, you're right," she declared with delight. It was so well camouflaged none of them had noticed it before. As one, they ran over to the shelter. Braxis knelt to cover their right side, while Kes echoed his movements to the left. Singh readied his weapon as he and Selena approached. She stood to one side and threw aside the tent flap while Kes braced himself, weapon ready, facing the opening. For a moment no one spoke. It was empty.

Kes rose to his feet and walked over to a small dead campfire. Kneeling on one knee he held his hand open above the ashes and then sifted them through his fingers. "These are cold. I'd say that no one's been here for quite a while. Franks and the others could be anywhere but at least we know for sure we're on the right track."

"One moment," Arthur held out his fist and opened it. In it was a small box made of the same ceramic material as his skin. As they watched the lid popped open and small metallic insects flew out.

"The bees," Selena said.

Those small golden machines rose straight upwards and for a moment remained in mid-air, before shooting off suddenly in all directions. Arthur's gaze followed them as he said, "We may as well make camp, there's everything we need right here. If they are around trust me, my bees will find them, and of course there's always the remote chance they could come back on their own anyway."

"Agreed. Kes, clean out that fire pit," Selena ordered. "Braxis, search their tent, see if you can find any clues. Singh, I want you to do a perimeter check. Arthur, go with him. When you're all done put your own tents up. We could be here for quite a while."

Later, when they'd made their own camp, Arthur went out again. After strolling around peering into all kinds of things he disappeared into the tree but returned after about thirty minutes. "I need you all to come with me," he said, "though it's a bit of a walk. The bees have found something. Unfortunately it's not our friends."

With Arthur leading the way through the forest they finally came to a clearing and stood before a large grass-covered mound, with dirt exposed on one side to the elements. Hundreds of Caretakers were working away at it feverishly, so it boiled as if it were covered with ants.

"What' that?" Selena asked. "It looks like a dig site."

"Aye, it sure does," Kes replied. "Those Caretakers appear to be covering it back up again and what are those things they're carrying, sticks?"

No one said anything for a while, and then Arthur spoke. "I'd say that those are bones."

They turned to him as one, their faces whitening.
"Of what?" Selena asked.

The warm and gentle wind bought a subtle, cloying scent from the blood trees. "I'd say it's this planet's original occupants," Arthur replied.

Selena turned to him, stunned. "How could you possibly know that?"

Arthur turned his pristine ceramic face to her. "According to the bees those remains were buried with advanced technology, which the caretakers are now reburying. It appears that there are a great many other similar sites showing up around us on the bees sensors. These scans also show countless ancient ruins of what appear to be cities. According to the bees estimates this grave could hold five hundred thousand bodies and, judging by the sheer number of the burial sites they've detected one can imagine there's a great many dead here. I'd say what we're looking at is evidence of genocide."

*****

No one wanted to look more closely at the mass grave, so they returned to the camp and sat around the fire which Kes had made with deadwood and then lit to combat the cold, as the day drew on and the temperature dropped. They ate silently, each alone with their thoughts. At length Singh finished and put down his plate. Then he held his cup before him in both hands, as if savouring the smell of the fresh coffee and enjoying the warmth.

"If the ForeRunners built the rabbit holes then it makes sense this is one of their worlds," he began, "but if that's the case then what's with all the bodies?"

"Could be the Manta arrived suddenly and killed them, and then left before the ForeRunners returned," Kes offered.

Arthur held a cup of the coffee too, staring into the hot depths but not drinking. "Or it could be a world they wrestled from the Manta after the bugs murdered the original inhabitants."

"None of that makes sense," Selena replied. "The ForeRunners lost that war, remember? So, if they'd wrested this place from the Manta, as you suggest, then the Manta would have come back and reclaimed it when they finally won. This all points to these dead inhabitants, whatever they were, either dying before the ForeRunners got here…"

"Or the ForeRunners themselves killed them," Kes continued for her. "But why would they do something like that?"

One of the sentry guns suddenly burped into life. Instantly they snatched up their weapons and dived into what cover they could, as a monstrous horse-like reptilian creature three times their height raced out of the blood trees straight towards them. With a deafening scream its awesome jaws opened, displaying arm-length and razor-sharp teeth. Then it staggered and bellowed as its body was ripped apart by hundreds of high explosive, armour piecing rounds. The creature stopped, gave a long drawn out groan and collapsed with a sickening thud. The sentry gun fell silent.

After a moment's pause they stood and walked over to examine the creature's body. At a murmured instruction from Selena, Braxis played the beam of his slicer backwards and forwards over the body, turning it to ashes, while the others returned to their seats. All of them cradled their weapons, peering into the darkness that was falling around them. Before long nothing remained of the creature except burns on the grass and a fine ash drifting on the now chill wind.

"Jesus, did you see those teeth," Braxis said, taking a seat and putting his weapon down beside him. "It had a mouth like a chainsaw."

"I want two of you on guard at all times tonight," Selena ordered, her breath puffed white. "Kes, you're with me, Singh with Braxis. You two have the first watch, six hours each shift."

"What about me?" Arthur inquired. "I can stay awake all night. There's no need for you to stand guard, you could all take a rest."

"You do that, supplement the others," she replied. Climbing to her feet she turned her back on him and entered her tent, the flaps closing behind her.

*****

The sunrise through the frost covered blood trees was spectacular. The scenery changed rapidly from a sea of frozen darkness to one of blood-red, as the warmth of the sun chased away the chill of the night and revealed the natural colour of the trees.

"What the..." Kes pointed towards a cat-sized flying creature that looked somewhat like a drifting jellyfish. It alighted gently on one of the branches and stared at them through myriad gleaming eyes that grew out of its body on long thin wavering stalks. Then with a sudden shriek the creature disappeared, as one of the mesh-leaves snapped shut around it and sucked it squirming into the tree.

"Are you thinking what I am?" Singh asked. "That thing looked intelligent. If it was and came from around here then it would surely have known not to sit where it did, which suggests it's from someplace else."

Before anyone could say anything else Arthur leapt to his feet and his pale countenance broke into a grin. "We need to go, right now. I've despatched a bee to bring Harding and the Skimmer through the tunnel. Forgive me, Captain, but this is important. We've found Franks and Amanda!"

The bees found their friends eighty miles away and, while Selena agreed with Arthur's decision, she wished he'd consulted her first. It seemed churlish, however, to tell him off. Particularly in front of the others, but she was determined to have a word with him when they had a quiet moment.

Harding arrived within thirty minutes. As the transport set down beside them he looked around at the tent and the burn marks on the grass and the trees damaged by gunfire from the sentry gun. "Looks like I missed the party."

"We'll fill you in later," Selena looked at Arthur. "You drive, I want us there soonest. Now move."

*****

"It was the smoke and heat from their fire that attracted the bees," Arthur informed them, as he guided the skimmer over the treetops. "We're just about there now."

As he spoke their small craft slowed and then lowered to the ground beside a small campfire and a skimmer that lay close to some ancient ruins. Amanda and Franks ran up to their craft waving and grinning insanely, as they all climbed out. To Selena's surprise Franks ignored her proffered hand and hugged her, his rough brown beard tickling her face.

"Selena, I'm so glad to see you." He grinned, hugged her again and then shook hands with the others, but his blue eyes widened in astonishment at the sight of Arthur. "Our skimmer died on us and we've no idea why. Bizarrely the same thing happened to the radio equipment."

"Singh, check it out."

"Have you any news about Hope?" Amanda asked.

"Sorry, not yet. We'd hoped you'd found her," Selena replied.

"No, we were doing a wide sweep and hoping she'd hear the skimmer and try to attract our attention. Then we saw these ruins and stopped to investigate," Franks said. "We were intending to return to our base camp, but when we came back here we found that the skimmer's power units were completely drained and the solar chargers had no effect on them at all, or the radios come to that."

"I'm so glad you found us," Amanda added. "One more day and we'd have been forced to walk back, even if there are nasties out there."

Singh climbed out of their vehicle. "This thing is royally screwed, but I can't figure out why. It'll probably

~ 42 ~

be a damn good idea to get out of here pronto, before the same thing happens to our own machine."

"Agreed," Selena said. "Come on, let's go."

Franks and Amanda grabbed their equipment and tossed it aboard the skimmer, leaping agilely over the sides and sitting down gratefully. Once back at the camp they were soon tucking into hot stew and thick crusty bread, rustled up by Braxis.

"I've a question for you," Selena began. "What can you tell us about the dig? Arthur tells me that there appears to be millions of bodies buried there, and those caretakers are very intent on covering it all up."

"Yeah, we noticed that," Franks replied through a mouthful of food. "We spotted the site shortly after we arrived. It was already partially exposed and the caretakers were working away like crazy, that's why they were coming through the rabbit holes empty handed. We tried to clear some of it and take a look, but they kept covering it back up again. We were hoping it would provide some clues as to what happened here, with regards to the ruins, and possibly even what might have happened to Hope. We thought she might have wandered in there somehow and become trapped.

"Just before we set off to the ruined city the caretakers intensified what they were doing, no idea why. Perhaps it's a religious thing, respect of the dead, or perhaps even a fear of whatever killed them. We still don't understand what uncovered the bodies in the first place and it didn't really matter that much at the time. I expect a research team will be sent here soon. In the meantime our prime concern is to search for Hope."

"I have a thought about the power loss on your skimmer," Singh said, changing the subject. "It strikes me that's quite an effective defence. If you're holed up in a city fighting for your lives and your enemy loses all power in their weapons and vehicles, then that could make a hell of a difference to the battle."

"Yes, but turn that on its head," Kes replied. "What if it was the other side who had those weapons? If they could drain the defenders power sources, it would soon be game over."

They spoke for a while and then Selena suggested the exhausted Franks and Amanda retire to their tent, reassuring them the bees would continue the search while they slept and they'd be woken immediately if there was any news. Selena and Kes took first watch, Singh and Braxis the second. When Selena awoke in the morning it was to find Singh gently shaking her shoulder. He held out a cup of tea and watched her accept it and blow on the hot liquid, before taking a sip.

"I've got something to show you," he said.

"What?" she asked, stretching with a slight groan and ignoring the sleeping bag as it slipped aside and revealed her bare breasts. She took another sip of the near scalding liquid and then put the cup down. Swinging her legs out she stood on the groundsheet and began to dress. The morning air was damp and mysterious, filled with the cloying musk of wild flowers and Selena found herself relaxing.

"You just need to come with me," Singh replied, shaking his head from side to side while an odd grin played over his lips. "You're going to love this."

Rubbing at her face with bare hands, Selena followed him out of the tent and across the clearing. She was desperate for a shower, but could always wash after. The others, apart from Braxis who remained behind to guard the camp, trailed along behind them. In moments they all stood before the lines of caretaker machines working away at the dig site.

"Watch," Singh said, and then called loudly through cupped hands. "Hey, I'm hungry get me an apple."

~ 44 ~

One of the machines froze for a moment or two and then turned to face them, while the others carried on as before. As the stream of its fellows carried countless baskets of dirt down into the dark, gaping hole this one suddenly scuttled away and quickly came back with an apple. Sitting on its back legs it rose up to waist height and handed the apple to Singh, before returning to work with the other machines. Singh's eyes twinkled as he took a large bite of the crunchy green fruit and chewed, aromatic juice dripping down his chin.

Selena frowned. "How did you do that?"

"You know me," Singh replied, swallowing. "I just thought it funny to ask one of them to do it, but I was amazed when it complied. It's obvious they understand our language, but I've no idea why they'd obey us."

"My God," Amanda gasped from behind Selena. "Do you realise what this means?"

"What? Are you all right, hon?" Franks asked, putting his hand on her arm and turning her to face him, worriedly.

Amanda shrugged him off. "Hey," she called loudly. Again one of the caretakers stopped and faced them. "We've lost my daughter, Hope. Go and find her for me."

With that a dozen or so other machines stopped and joined their comrade facing Selena and the others. Remaining still for a few moments they then turned as one and marched off into the trees.

Franks shook his head disbelievingly. "Surely it can't be that simple."

The caretakers didn't return for the rest of the day and Selena and her party spent some time combing the area. Early next morning Selena was patrolling the perimeter when she heard, "Captain, come quickly."

It was Jack who'd shouted from the other side of the camp, and they all ran up to him before stopping to stare in disbelief, as a group of the machines marched out of the jungle interlocked into one solid platform, on which a young girl sat half asleep in a lotus position.

"Hope!" Amanda shrieked, and ran to greet her daughter.

Chapter Three

Van Pluy looked up from his desk as Selena entered his office back at the citadel. "Report, Captain. Where are Franks and the others?"

"All three are in sick bay, Sir, being checked out. They seem fine, but Hope isn't saying much. I've asked her several times what happened, why she left in the first place and why she was gone so long, but all she can remember is falling. That's it."

"Falling?"

"Aye, Sir. All we know is while she was on Eden Hope decided to go for a walk, bearing in mind she's only four. Arthur's guessing she saw the caretakers acting peculiarly and followed them into the rabbit hole, as did her mother and father after her. When Hope arrived in what we now call Arcadia, she fell down an incline and hurt herself. She just remembers waking up as the caretakers were carrying her into the base camp, after Amanda asked them to find her for us."

"Hmm, does she have any injuries?"

"None that I could see. I've arranged for her to be checked out, just to be sure."

Van Pluy's fingers danced over his keyboard and then he peered into the small screen in front of him. He leant forward suddenly, intent. Then he sighed heavily. "It's just as well you did. Take a look at this." The display flicked onto a larger wall-screen on the wall, to Selena's left.

Selena felt herself go rigid with shock. "What...?" she gasped, staring at the body scan.

"It appears," the admiral replied, sitting back in his chair, "that our young friend has had all her bones replaced by the same glass-like alloy the ForeRunners had. This means either Hope was badly injured during her fall and the caretakers carried out medical procedures to help her, or this isn't our Hope at all."

"What about Franks and Amanda? I had them checked out as well. After all they were there for a long time too."

The screen changed to show Franks's and Amanda's reports. Van Pluy relaxed visibly and said, "No, they're okay, normal from what I can see, although we need to get them to sickbay to run more tests. Eventually I'm going to have to tell them about Hope though. God knows what they're going to say. Imagine losing your child for all this time, and then getting her back to find she might not be who you think she is. In the meantime, there's a transport leaving with reinforcements for Capulet in two days. I want you and your team on it."

Selena's eyes narrowed and her lips thinned. "The Queen won't have forgotten what I did. She's an untrustworthy evil bitch. What's to stop her having me killed when I get there?"

The admiral rested his elbows on his desk, steepled his fingers and looked at her thoughtfully. "She's signed up to our treaty. If she does anything wrong we'll get you out and walk away from that world, and she knows it. We're still Humanity's best fighting force. We may be down to five battalions but we're building our numbers back up again."

Selena gritted her teeth, fighting back the rage building in her. "I knew the Federation of Man bastards hurt us but not that badly."

"There are still things you don't need to be aware of, Captain. To be frank, with you going into enemy territory and fighting alongside those backstabbing bastards then you really don't need-to-know. Now, you'll join the Second Regiment, Fifth Century."

"I've got one hundred men?"

"Yes, but, as I said, Kes and the others are to go with you, including Lieutenant Jones. We'll soon see what this new Arthur is made of, if you excuse the pun. Your Commanding Officer is one of ours, General Magki. Apparently he's of Korean descent. His second in command is a regular by the name of Colonel Bob Matthews, a good man. Do you have any questions?"

"What are the battalion's current orders?"

"To kill the enemy, something you appear to excel at. That's all there is to it. Capulet City's still standing, the charged defensive metal ring around it has kept them fairly secure, the Manta haven't been able to get past it. We've taken this on board and have recommended all allied world re-instigate the design in their cities. We've also ensured our own citadels and bases re-adopt their original design, which included it. You'll be billeted in Capulets Arena, which we're using as a barracks for the time being. Oh, and there's one other thing."

"Admiral?"

"I know your feelings on the matter but Capulet's Queen is currently still alive. Just make sure she is when you leave."

Selena studied him for a moment, her face devoid of emotion, and the admiral stared straight back at her. "Yes, Sir," she replied, tight lipped.

He leant forward suddenly and jabbed a manicured finger at Selena. "I mean it, Dillon. I know you have an axe to grind, but it will have to wait. As you pointed out, in the old days you'd never have gone back. We're fighting alongside the Federation of Man on this one and we need to do things by the book. While there's a temporary truce in place we'll work together against the aliens. I don't need the media making the most of any indiscretion. I have enough problems as it is. Do I make myself clear?"

"Absolutely."

"Good, then you're dismissed. Oh, and by the way, good luck."

"Thank you, Sir."

As Selena closed the door behind her she stopped in mid-step, jaw dropping open. "Kotes, what are you doing here?"

He grinned. "If you remember you have a shuttle that belongs to me. Singh 'borrowed' it to rescue you and I'd quite like it back. As it happens, the admiral's ordered me to take you and the others to Capulet. I promise not to take a detour on the way, like I did the last time I took you somewhere."

"Thank you, Lieutenant, I'd really appreciate that."

"Good." His grin came back. "Now, could you tell me where I can find Singh? He owes me some supplies, that beggar drank all my whiskey."

*****

Despite expectations the *Magellan's* journey to Capulet went without issue and their time was spent on hard physical training and re-familiarisation with weapons. Before long Selena and the others found themselves on her home world, somewhere she thought she'd never see again. Kotes met them on the gangway, as they disembarked. He shook their hands and looked askance at Arthur, as if unsure what to do, but Arthur resolved the situation by simply ignoring him and walking straight past without offering his hand. Selena offered Kotes an apologetic look, shouldered her belongings and assault rifle and strode down the gangway after Arthur. Once on the tarmac she stopped and looked around. It had been a long time since she'd been here but the old city hadn't changed much. It was still surrounded by a sea of green grass and the forest, yet somehow smelt like a dusty hell-hole. The spaceport was within the tall crenulated city wall, with its countless colourful flags and pennants fluttering in the warm, dry wind. Even from where they were she could see a lot more gun emplacements and men manning them.

"Are you all right?" Singh whispered. "It must be weird being here again. By the way, it looks like we have a welcome committee."

On the tarmac in front of the *Magellan* was a small diminutive officer of Asian descent. His black uniform was impeccable and he saluted smartly as Selena strode up to him.

Selena returned his salute. "You are?"

"Lieutenant Rai, Ma'am."

Selena proffered her hand, which he shook, almond eyes crinkling with delight. "Now, if you don't mind," she continued, "I'd like to see my quarters."

Rai led them to a skimmer and once aboard they rose above the buildings and were taken straight over the busy streets and market places directly to the arena. Selena felt her eyes drawn to the old stone court house, and the cell in which she'd been imprisoned all those years ago before being taken away for induction into the Penal corps. Their craft slowed and landed. As they climbed out she glanced at Arthur, then paused and peered more closely at him. "Hey Arthur, are you all right? You look kind of swollen, and you're walking a bit stilted."

The once gleaming face looked somewhat dulled, but he immediately said: "I'm okay, Captain. I don't think this new body's used to trips through space."

"Yeah, well, I guess not, though that seems a bit odd, after all you're a goddamned robot. It's not like I can get a doctor to check you out or anything, although maybe a mechanic. Let me know if it gets any worse, and if there's anything I can do."

Arthur nodded, his sapphire gaze took in the multitude of pennants fluttering in the warm breeze on the city's battlements, "Oh, trust me Ma'am, I will."

*****

"The arena hasn't changed much, apart from all the tents on the grass where we used to hold the events," Selena said to Singh. "You guys unpack. I've a few things to do."

Her eyes caught the massive grey-stone entrance with its colonial crest. Instantly Selena saw her mother standing there all those years ago, her white gown flapping gently in the breeze and giving tantalising glimpses of her superb, well-toned body to those so far below. The pennants fluttered as she raised her arms and spoke, her voice carrying over the arena as she told all those before her the Queen was responsible for the death of Raynor, her husband and the one person she'd ever loved. Then Selena saw her mother fall to her death from that precipice once again. Shaking off the memories she turned away, so her friends couldn't see the tears in her eyes.

Selena dropped her belongings off in the chameleon tent assigned to her and reported to HQ. There she found her senior officers were both away, but they'd left orders for her and the troops to join them in the morning.

Returning to her tent she unpacked, took a shower in the ablutions block and, once refreshed, told Rai to muster the men. Introducing herself she briefed them on their orders and inspected them, finding herself pleased with the results. She, Singh and the others ate dinner in the mess tent before she excused herself and decided to get an early night. When she returned to the tent and undressed, it took a while for her to get to sleep. When she did Selena's dreams were filled with her parents. It was about two a.m. when Singh woke her.

"Captain, we've got a problem. You'd better come and take a look."

"What is it?" she asked, pulling on her clothes before joining him outside.

"It's Arthur. You need to see this, Ma'am."

They ran the short distance under a clear night sky filled with a profusion of brilliant stars, while the small twin-moons, Romeo and Juliet, bathed all with their soft warm glow. As they entered Arthur's tent, Selena stopped short, the breath catching in her throat. Arthur lay still, like a cast-aside toy on his bunk. He looked swollen, his body plating disjointed and cracked. The once pristine white armour had turned a horrible greyish colour and started to lift in places. Selena approached him and looked more closely. What was that underneath those lifting scabs of ceramic? Her eyes widened, *it couldn't be*. Kneeling on the groundsheet she reached down and tugged gently at a piece of the plating. It came free with a rasping, sticky sound. Behind her she heard Singh gasp, as he too realised what it was that lay beneath the plating.

Human skin.

Urgently they pulled away more of the material, until they'd revealed a whole left forearm, and then a hand. There was a smell of rank, rotten cheese – enough to make them retch. Then they noticed Arthur's mask was lifting too and, reaching forward, they carefully lifted that away as well. It came free reluctantly with a sucking, slurping sound, as if they were pulling a boot free from deep gelatinous mud. Selena took a tissue from her pocket and wiped away some of the yellow mucous that lay underneath like congealed pus, revealing the sleeping face of the Arthur they knew so well. His ragged breathing changed suddenly, increasing and becoming more robust. He grunted and raised his freed hand to rub away more of the disgusting goo. Long strands of the snot-like gunge dribbled from his face onto the bed. Then he opened those blue eyes, and looked at them with surprise.

"Hello, Captain. Looks like I have some explaining to do."

*****

"Are you're telling me," Selena demanded, interrupting Arthur as he sat on the side of his bed, dressed in one of Singh's spare tee-shirt and shorts, both of which were far too big for him, "that when we first found the device which activated the rabbit holes, there were data crystals there and you didn't declare them?"

"Ermm, yeah, I'm afraid so. I didn't realise what they were at first. I just kind of picked them up and put them in my pocket, while I was brushing off all the other dust and debris off the device. It was only a couple of days later that I remembered them and cleaned them up."

"Don't bullshit me," Selena snapped, her eyes flashing as she poked him in the chest. "You've said yourself you don't forget anything."

He looked guilty and shrugged. "Like I said, I didn't realise what they were. When I did we were already aboard the *Magellan* and on our way to the *Dutch Lady*. There was a lot of time to kill once we'd settled in, I was fascinated and wanted to fully investigate what this all was before I said anything. Yes, okay I admit once I'd figured out what the crystals were and how to download their information I kept it all to myself, but that wasn't until I was absolutely sure of what it was I'd found. Even when I tried it I didn't really know what I was doing and had to work it out as I went. I thought it was just a machine my consciousness could be downloaded to. How was I to know it would build a clone of me inside it, or as the body matured the shell would die and eventually peel away."

"You didn't report it and you should have. You know that."

"Yes, you're quite right, but I was intrigued and the journey to Mantis allowed me the time to start the research I needed. I certainly didn't expect to be bloody killed! I'd already sent the plans for the mechanical body to Franks, asking him to keep it to himself and arrange for it to be built as part of a secret project. The poor guy was so thankful for our help on Loreen that he did exactly what I asked and kept quiet about it, apart from those he personally involved in the project to help him.

"It was only just prior to our attacking run I downloaded my 'memories' into the transference device that I'd built into Henry. That's honestly the last thing I remember and, as I said before, Henry was destroyed when the device activated and I've no idea why; so all of my research had been lost."

"Where are the data crystals now?"

"Probably still with the old me, buried back at the crash site." He rubbed some more of the gel away and flicked it towards the floor with his fingers.

"I don't believe a word of this, Arthur. It's bullshit and all too coincidental. We'll talk about this later. In the meantime, let's get you over to medical."

Luckily the bunks were designed to be used as stretchers, when needed. They called a couple of guards, who soon had Arthur in the medical tent.

An hour later Selena looked at his scans. Speaking to Arthur over her shoulder she said, "It says here you're in incredibly good health. You certainly don't need those spectacles you used to wear anymore, although why you never got your eyes fixed in the first place is beyond me."

"I've always been a bit funny about my eyes. I can't stand anyone playing with them, makes me go all cold."

"These scans also show your bone structure is made from the same glass-like material the ForeRunners used, the same as Hope's. Care to explain that one away?"

Arthur pursed his lips. "Do you recall the DNA scanner that allowed us access to the rabbit holes when we first discovered them? I believe they granted us access because they recognised us as some sort of descendent from the ForeRunners, because our DNA matched theirs. It would also explain why the caretakers brought Singh an apple, and Hope back when Amanda asked them to. It may be they see our requests as orders."

"Ah," Selena replied, light dawning. "Hope said the last thing she recalled was falling. So when the caretakers found her and realised she was injured they must have repaired her, thinking she was a ForeRunner."

She fell silent and looked closely at Arthur. "If this is all true then the question is whether you two really are human, or something else entirely?"

*****

Returning to her room Selena called the admiral. Luckily, Van Pluy was still up and answered quickly.

"Report," he ordered.

She told him about the developments with Arthur and then about Hope, finishing with, "My concerns, Sir, are whether these really are Arthur and Hope, or are they really some kind of ForeRunner copy? In either case, can they be trusted?"

Van Pluy puffed his cigar into vermillion life, blowing a grey cloud to one side. "Those are good points you've raised, Captain. So what do you suggest?"

"There isn't a lot I can do, Sir, except clap him in irons and at the moment he doesn't deserve it. The other thing is the Forerunners and Manta fought against each other, so I'd rather have him at my side helping us than rotting somewhere away in a forgotten cell, or even being dissected for that matter."

"Agreed. Okay, keep him with you at all times and watch him like a hawk. I'll arrange for Hope to be monitored constantly. I have to admit, Selena, I'm still troubled by those skeletons you found on Arcadia. Something doesn't add up and alarm bells are ringing. There's also the issue of the power loss, the last thing we want is more people marooned over there."

"It's bothering me too, Sir, but I'm sure we'll get to the bottom of it eventually. I've thought about this clinical

~ 56 ~

immortality, or whatever we're going to call it. The ForeRunners lost their war with the Manta and I'm wondering whether they invented this technology as a means to keep their numbers up. If you think about it, as they lost ships all they had to do was upload the latest version of their memories into these robotic bodies beforehand and their numbers would replete constantly."

"I guess that makes sense, but then anything's possible."

"In the meantime, Sir, I'm to report with my men to the General in the morning. It's two a.m. here already, so with your permission I'd like to go get some rest."

"Your orders are online, read them. In the meantime, Captain, you're excused. Good luck, sleep well and keep me posted."

*****

Early the next morning with all the men mustered and ready, Selena inspected them and then told them to sit. She remained standing, hands behind her back, and looked them over one-by-one. Selena informed them that, at midday, half their battalion would attack one of the enemy nests and the other half a second one. At the same time Federal troops would attack the remaining two nests. It was hoped this coordinated attack would prevent each alien base from reinforcing the others. She turned to Singh, who was standing to her left.

"Lieutenant Lacey, you were involved in a battle on Theta before it was lost to the enemy and then destroyed. Is there anything you'd like to share with us? We've all studied the data but a first-hand report would be helpful."

Singh stepped forward and addressed the troops. "As I expect you know, the enemy shields hang like a blanket over their bases, protecting them from above but leaving the sides vulnerable — hence the best way to attack them is from the ground. These bases will no doubt have anti-ship beams. The shields will drop to allow them to fire at any craft in orbit before springing back up again. Apart from those, and projectile weapons, there will be air-mines and anti-personnel darts, then there's the Manta themselves. Don't give or expect any quarter, the aliens have no concept of mercy what-so-ever. When you've shot something make sure it stays down. Keep on shooting at it until it stops moving, or I guarantee it will crawl after you and tear your legs off." He noticed several of the troops blanche and finished with, "On that happy note, good luck. If you bear in mind what I've said, you'll be fine."

When Singh stepped back behind Selena again she glanced at him quickly, the twinkle in her eye letting him know he'd done well, and then continued. "We need to exterminate these nests as quickly as possible. So, don't stop to think about it, just kill anything that moves except your comrades. If we don't do this now they'll breed more soldiers, and we can't afford that. For those of you who don't know, when the *Dutch Lady* was on route to attack Mantis we discovered they'd captured our spy and research ship *Scott*. The intelligence the enemy gathered from that vessel revealed why they'd been unable to grow their crops anywhere else but on their home planet, Mantis. There was a rare element in its soil that it needed to grow. Capulet also has it, hence why they're here, so the chances are they're now growing those crops underground and breeding their warriors again, so we need to incinerate each and every farm they have. This way their soldiers we don't kill in battle starve to death."

As Selena spoke two heavily armoured black skimmers flew overhead, slowed and landed besides them. Before she could order them to embark on the craft Lieutenant Rai stepped forward.

"Captain, before we begin the men and I have something for you," He presented her with a large, slightly curved knife in a skin sheath. "It's a kukri, the fighting blade of my people. I'd be honoured if you'd carry it."

Stunned, Selena accepted it and attached the heavy blade to her belt. As she went to draw it the Lieutenant put his hand on her arm.

"Ma'am, we believe the blade needs to taste blood each time it's drawn, even if it's your own."

Selena nodded her thanks, not sure she'd be happy about nicking herself with the blade each time she cleaned or sharpened it. She saw Arthur had gotten hold of a machine gun from somewhere but decided to make nothing of it. He was a damn good fighter and she needed him on board.

"Load 'em up people," she said, savagely. "There's a battle brewing and it isn't going to wait for us."

Chapter Four

The alien nest was shaped like a small concrete volcano and lay under a cloudy, threatening morning sky in a forest clearing several hundred meters across. They could just see a few of the buildings scattered around it were egg-shell white, while others a transparent yet opulent blue or emerald-green. Some were shaped like bubbles resting on the ground. There were also tall pyramids and even a few that looked like rectangular jewels balanced insanely on one corner, suggesting to the onlookers that they were going to fall over at any moment. Above the building lay a shimmering transparent cover that Selena instantly recognised as a shield.

"I've had nightmares for years about the last one of these Bryn and I attacked," Singh commented, as a wind smelling of rain rose slightly sending waves through his short hair. "You'd think the powers-that-be could have come up with some kind of plan to fire a missile into the middle of the enemy base, rather than waste lives."

"They've tried it. Their defences just take them out, even salvos of them. Soldiers are better, they fight back," Selena replied, double checking the magazine on her weapon and her grenade launcher were full. "The only proven way is a ground attack, we fight our way in and plant a thermal bomb and get the hell out. That'll turn this whole place into glass."

"Just as well we brought some with us then, otherwise they might have been tempted to use nukes and they've been banned planet-side for decades, ever since the terrorist attack on Rigelon Prime which killed thousands of colonists," Kes said. "You'd think the powers that be would want to capture at least one of the Manta bases. You never know what we might learn from them."

"No way, there could be eggs or young ones hidden anywhere. It's better to glass everything, rather than have them bursting out of the walls when we least expect it."

Selena reported over the battle-net they were ready and turned to her troops. "Once we're in close enough, I'll send a signal to drop the gravpacks and proceed on foot. They'll hinder us otherwise, and we can collect them once we're done."

"There's a lot of air mines," Singh reported with a low whistle, as he looked through his binoculars, watching the small spheres patrolling the enemy camp.

"Shouldn't be too bad, the droids have been ordered to take them out," Selena replied quietly, taking cover beneath a large, wide-leaved bush as soldiers slipped through the trees around them. She took another look through her binoculars.

A few minutes later the order to attack came and the droids rose and launched themselves towards the enemy base, guns blazing.

"Go!" Selena shouted and all around her troops shot into the air and swarmed towards the enemy's installation.

Beams from the circular battledroids flashed towards the enemy mines, which exploded with mind-numbing explosions but not before many of them already locked onto and were arrowing towards the humans. The blasts scattered body parts in all directions. The air-mines totally ignored the droids, leaving them to the blaze of gunfire coming from the alien dwellings. Then homing-darts slipped from the structures and sped towards the troops. Despite all efforts, the human losses began to mount. Short, rapid beams of fire scythed through the human ranks and also battered the attacking droids.

"Forget everything else, focus on the mines!" Selena bellowed, her machine gun juddering in her arms as they flew over the ground towards the enemy base. The mines exploded in their hundreds, scattering shrapnel in all directions, and she breathed a sigh of relief when the last she could see detonated.

"Charge!" She yelled, increasing the velocity on her gravpack. Her unit rocketed towards the enemy base, shooting at everything that moved and hosing fire at the weapon emplacements. Suddenly the Manta boiled out of the top of the nest, spilling from dark tunnels on its side and raced towards them like a tide of black ink.

"Gravpacks off," she ordered. Slowing, she landed and shrugged out of her own gravpack, her gut wrenching in disbelief at the sheer number of Manta streaming towards them. All around her the men landed and followed suit. They knelt or lay down in the dirt, took what cover they could, and let rip with their weapons. Another volley of homing darts sped towards them but the droids took these out easily. Then the enemy beam weapons began to focus solely on the droids, whose heavy weapons were now trying to take out the enemy emplacements. The droid for Selena's century exploded like a bomb only a short distance away killing two of her men, chunks of its armour plating narrowly missing her. Next to Selena a soldier cried out and she turned her head to look, as a dark-red stain spread over the woman's tunic. Selena's eyes rose to the woman's face before the dart that had buried itself in her chest detonated, ripping her apart like an over-ripe fruit. Selena wiped something warm and wet from her face and turned back to face the enemy and carried on firing.

The praying mantis-like aliens were now only a short distance away. Their mechanical top set of eyes were each scanning different directions, while their four organic purple plum-sized eyes lay below them, reminding her of those belonging to a blowfly. Despite their massive losses the Manta kept coming. They simply climbed over their fallen comrades, stretched talons and mandibles towards their human prey and ran at them, uttering shrill keening cries that Selena hadn't heard before. Multi-coloured bandoliers brimming with armament festooned their chests, and each claw held a separate weapon which they fired in all directions. It was utter bedlam, a blood-splattered screaming madness that only the insane could imagine.

"Grenades!" Selena yelled. Setting the shotgun nestling beneath her machine gun to grenade launcher, she pulled the trigger and launched a stream of the powerful projectiles straight into the enemy ranks, grimacing as the explosions tore them to pieces. Besides her, those with slicers or microwave lasers pulled homing grenades from their belts, tugged at the pins and lobbed them towards the enemy swarm. Automatically the grenades 'friend-or-foe' kicked in and their small drives drove the weapons straight at the enemy, exploding and scattering body parts to all sides. More grenades followed, like a flock of deadly birds, and between these and the assault rifles hammering and flashing the enemy ranks dwindled.

"Forward," Selena shouted, climbing to her feet and running towards the nest, firing as she went.

She leapt over fallen bodies of the enemy, Singh, Kes, Arthur and the others at her side. Lieutenant Rai was smashed backwards in mid-stride, a gaping hole where his chest had been. Then a fresh surge of Manta poured from the tunnels at the base of the nest, only to be slaughtered in their thousands as the humans' sustained fire slammed into them. Besides her Arthur knelt down, a machine gun held tight into his shoulder blazing away. A piece of shrapnel tore his cheek open, but he ignored it and carried on shooting. Then he was up, running besides her, firing as they went. To her right a soldier leapt over a fallen Manta, only for the nightmare beast to snatch her out of the air. Screaming and struggling the soldier pulled her knife and stabbed the Manta repeatedly, until the creature bit her head clean off and spat it out to roll away over the grass. Selena dived, rolled and came back to her feet with her weapon in her arms hosing rounds into the deadly creature.

Selena led the others into the tunnels, shooting at anything non-human moving and only pausing long enough to reload. They spilled out into a large chamber, filled from wall to wall with wide transparent platforms, one above the other. They brimmed with interlocking purple-veined, bluish-green plants stretching up a web-like material from one platform to another and then up to the roof tapering off far above them. Each platform supported the one above it with a multitude of thick transparent beams through which a strange and noxious looking liquid pumped. Those platforms were like layers of mini forests through which little could be seen.

"Braxis, Kes, get over here!" she bellowed. As they panted up to her she fired more grenades into a band of the enemy that peered from around the platforms and took pot shots at them. She grinned with satisfaction as she blasted them from their feet and their gore splattered the walls behind them. "Kes, use your microwave laser. I want all the vegetation incinerated. Braxis, use your slicer, burn the lot."

The alien crops were soon sheets of flame, crackling and roaring while black smoke whipped towards the ceiling and then away, drawn no doubt by some kind of vent. More soldiers fell as the aliens attacked again and again. The Manta streamed from unseen tunnels around the humans, desperate to save their crops. Then, quite suddenly, they were no more and the guns fell silent.

*****

The soldiers slowed their breathing, picked themselves up and patrolled back and forth, searching. Their guns barked occasionally, as they found enemy survivors. Then, with the perimeters secured, Selena finally counted her men.

"Thirty, is that all?" she asked. "Where's Harding?

"He got minced," Braxis replied, wincing. "He was standing right next to me once minute and was a cloud of blood the next. He couldn't have felt a thing, it was so damn quick."

Looking at him she could see blood and bits of human flesh adhering to his uniform, and noted a few shudders from those around her. To Selena's relief Singh, Kes and Arthur made it, although Kes had a large tear in his chest Singh was patching with a battle dressing and Arthur had a rip in his cheek they could see his teeth through. She left her men under Singh's command, as he in turn sat in the dirt having a shrapnel wound in his arm tended by a medic. With Kes, Braxis and a couple of heavies in tow Selena went to a meeting called by Colonel Matthews, in the central chamber of the nest. Above them were the platforms that once housed the alien crops, but were now filled with nothing but drifting ash.

"Hello, Dillon," the colonel said, holding out his hand. "Glad you made it. That was fine work back there. Your prompt action with the grenades broke the enemy's back."

His genuine smile relaxed Selena. She was quite taken by the man's warmth. His round face was framed by silvery hair. At five foot eight he was short, stocky, spoke in brusque tones and was the typical image of an army officer.

"Thank you, Colonel," she replied. "Do you know how the other attacks went?"

His smile faltered. "We succeeded at two of the other nests, but one of the regular army units was over-run and destroyed. I'm told there are no survivors at all. Luckily for us, the enemy chose to stay and defend the nest rather than send reinforcements to this one." He paused and looked around, before saying even more loudly, "Now you're all here, come with me. There's something I want to show you, but I warn you it's not pretty."

The colonel led them down several floors, and as they went a horrible stench began to assail their senses.

"God, what's that?" Selena asked.

Matthews neither answered nor looked at her, as they turned a last corner. The officers stopped mid-step and stared. In the wide open space there were hundreds of pens, all filled with transparent maggots of some kind that were as long as Selena's leg. They had thick leather-like skin and countless cilia, which writhed constantly. Their little dark mouths took chunks out of the pieces of plant trundling through the pens on conveyor belts. As the huge maggots chewed and gulped the food, it could easily be seen entering their bodies, bunching up in what could be termed a series of stomachs, before finally being ejected from their bodies in a dirty, watery stream.

Several of the officers besides Selena averted their eyes.

The colonel led them to a group of soldiers standing on one side of the room. Then he turned to them. "Prepare yourselves."

He led the way to the centre of the room, where they found themselves staring into a charnel pit filled with the bodies of cows, horses, dogs, cats and even Manta. Then to their despair they saw human bodies there too. It was all being fed into a mincing machine of some kind, the resulting mush being forced up through tubing, which led towards the platforms housing the alien crops.

"Christ," Selena said. "They're feeding both their dead and ours to their crops to make them grow, then eating the results."

"Actually, Ma'am," one of the other officers replied, "in many ways it makes perfect sense. If they lived a borderline existence on Mantis, as we suspect, then they'd have to make use of every nutrient they have, including their own dead. We can't blame them for that, particularly when we do something similar. If you think about it our ships on deep-space voyages recycle everything, even human remains and waste, and feed them to the hydroponic tanks too."

Selena noted in some of the pens the maggots had turned into deep-red, leathery ribbed chrysalises. About the room they were in dead Manta lay scattered, their arms filled with the chrysalises. "I guess they've been carrying them into other enclosures where they probably hatch and mature into adults, but where are they coming from?" she asked, staring into the writhing masses.

"Bellow us is yet another floor," the colonel replied. "We found worker Queens there giving birth to swarms of these things, live believe it or not. It's like they were shitting worms. At least we now know a lot more about the enemy than we did before. It's time to get the hell out of here, that thermal bomb's been planted and it's all set to blow."

*****

They were a mile away, when the bomb detonated. There was a blinding flash, and they all shielded their eyes as the ground shook with a deep growl-like rumble.

"Just like nukes but without the fallout," Arthur said, with a smile. "God, I love those things."

"You must have been a bundle of fun, as a kid," Singh observed, dryly.

"At least there's no risk of those beggars coming back to haunt us. All we need to worry about now is the last surviving nest," Braxis agreed. "The one the regulars fucked up on."

"You mean the ones the regulars died in. Well, we don't need to worry about that tonight." Selena touched her earpiece. "The general's ordering us back to the city, time for a rest. It's a new day tomorrow. I expect he'll get us to hit the last nest then."

*****

Back in the arena in Capulet City much later, Selena sat in the open with Arthur and Singh drinking a cold beer

~ 67 ~

while staring into the flames of a log fire built as a comfort against the night. They raised their eyes and watched as a troopship descended noisily from the dark, cloud filled sky. The roar from the cherry-red engines faded as it kissed the tarmac in the spaceport a short distance away.

"Wonder what they've got for us," Singh offered. "More beer?"

"That's probably the one with our first reinforcements from our new bases in the colonies," Selena replied. "It appears the admiral's efforts are finally paying off."

"Just as well," Arthur joined in. "Because at the rate we're losing people you're going to end up saluting yourself." He raised his beer. "Here's to our fallen, and to reinforcements."

"The metal staples in your cheek are an improvement," Selena remarked to Arthur. "A few inches to one side and you'll have needed Henry again. Looks like it's already starting to heal though, and that's pretty incredible."

"Yeah, so's the fact I can have a beer again and it isn't spilling through the side of my face," Arthur replied, downing his drink.

Just then an unearthly wail rose through the city. It sent a shiver down Selena's spine. Grabbing her gun she leapt to her feet.

"What's that?" Singh asked, standing beside her and looking around.

"The alarm," Selena replied. "The city's under attack."

Then a report came over Selena's battle net, informing everyone the Manta were in the city. All around them soldiers boiled into action, snatching up weapons and forming into squads before rushing off to wherever they were directed. Gunfire erupted and echoed through the streets, mingled with the crump of explosions that left fireballs raising into the night sky. Shrieking people ran through the streets, making the soldiers' job so much harder.

"They're in the city?" Singh bellowed, incredulously. "What about the perimeter?"

"Control says they dug under it."

Screams of pain and gunfire rent the night air. The lights throughout the city came on, bathing the arena and the buildings surrounding it. A few alleyways remained unlit and threatening. As alien shapes leapt from them they were mown down as the troops opened fire. In little over an hour only occasional shots from one quarter could be heard.

"Where's are those coming from?" Kes asked.

"Sounds like the palace," Selena replied. She looked towards the racket and sucked her lip. "Guess we better go see."

"Is that really a good idea?" Kes asked.

"I won't know until we get there. With luck the bitch is already dead."

"Erm, did I miss something?" Braxis said, eyebrows raised.

"Nothing you need worry about, yet," Kes answered. "Let's go."

They ran the half-mile or so to the palace, and found its gates hanging off. There they found dead guards and Manta everywhere, their bodies interwoven. The humans had fought with everything, from the most modern weapons to swords and knives, and even their bare hands.

"Why's aren't there any auto-guns here?" Braxis asked, as he and Kes took cover on one side of the wall while Selena, Arthur and Singh took the other.

"There's some inside but there used to be a lot more. I'd say most of those available were reclaimed and placed on the perimeter walls. I guess they didn't see this coming," Selena replied. Peering around the shattered entrance she ensured all was clear, "Let's go."

Even more torn, bleeding and burned bodies lay inside. Ignoring them they ran past smouldering buildings and through the gardens. From the corner of her eye Selena caught sight of a manhole cover. It bought back so many memories, for it was the exact one she and her team of assassins climbed out of during their assassination attempt.

As they ran across the grass a group of Manta leapt from the bushes and raced towards them. The team dropped to their knees, opened fire and took them out. Chitin was torn from the aliens' shells as the bullets slammed home. Then a microwave hit them and they exploded. Their rancid gore splashed over the bushes and trees, dispelling the sweet, cloying scent of the gardens.

The doors at the entrance to the passageway leading to the royal quarters had been torn off and the few auto-guns in the corridor beyond had taken a terrible toll of the enemy before the guns were disabled. Alien bodies lay piled up like a barrier, which they had to climb over, while ahead of them the few remaining humans and aliens battled hand to hand. The humans no match for the monstrous invaders, who began to batter at the door to the Queen's quarters.

The realising she had to stop them, no matter what, Selena shouted, "Pick your targets, open fire!" Once again the machine gun kicked in her arms and she knew that, no matter how they tried, they were bound to hit the defenders.

The others joined in, their weapons screaming as they sliced through both human and alien alike. Selena felt sick as she saw the defenders hammered from their feet by her bullets yet she little choice, the guards were too close to the enemy. But then knowing the crimes the guards perpetrated on behalf of the Queen, she had no great love for them either. At least it was some payback for the death of her parents, although she took no pleasure in it. Van Pluy told her to ensure the Queen was alive when she left the planet, and Selena had no choice but to follow those orders.

Changing grip on her weapon slightly she triggered her grenade launcher, the resulting explosion blowing both the remaining human defenders and their attackers to bits. As the smoke cleared she realised there was no combatants left alive, except one human guard who climbed slowly to his feet, a huge gash across his face. The piles of bodies protected him. Covered in blood and gore, with a blood-soaked sword in his hand, he stared in disbelief at the devastation around him, the piles of colleagues, dead friends and enemies. Behind him were the doors to the royal sleeping quarters, with their ornate and intricately designed golden birds fluttering over green leafed bamboo — at the feet of which the ivory dragons with blood-red eyes glared balefully remained undamaged — apart from the odd bullet or beam mark while occasional rivulets of gold trickled slowly towards the floor. Then the man's gaze met Selena's. His eyes blazing he raised his blade, screamed at the top of his voice and stepped forward.

"One more step and you're hamburger, drop it." Singh ordered.

The man froze, fury painting every look and body motion but he lowered the blade and did as he was told, his eyes promising revenge. The acrid scent of blood and weapon discharges filled the corridor, smoke drifted like pungent clouds. Selena walked up to the man and nodded at the dead Manta piled against his legs.

"Did you kill all of those?" She asked

"The guys and I did," he spat, "when the auto-guns failed but there were so many we couldn't kill them all, no matter how much we tried. Then you come along and murdered what was left of my friends anyway. What kind of bitch are you?"

"What's your name?"

"Ragnor."

"Well, Ragnor, two things. Firstly, you're a brave man and a good fighter. A lot of people would have run but you didn't and we could use a man like you. Secondly, don't ever call me a bitch again, it really pisses me off. If you do I'll cut your goddamned tongue out, you have my word on that. Now then, you've deliberately insulted a senior officer of the military and that's a crime for which I intend to ensure you're sentenced to the penal corps." Without another word she punched him square on the jaw, watching as his eyes glazed over and he slid to the floor unconscious.

Braxis stared at her. His lips moved but no words came out.

Selena returned his look. "What, have you got a problem Braxis?"

"No Ma'am, I sure haven't."

"I didn't think so," she replied, then gestured towards the human guards they'd help kill. "If the enemy had gotten through then the Manta would have slaughtered the Queen. Although in my book it couldn't happen to anyone more deserving, her death would be contrary to orders."

It was all that needed to be said.

Silence reigned for a moment. Cooling metal ticked, the smell of ozone stung their nostrils. Then they moved forward and checked the charred bodies. Beyond them a loud click came from the ornate door, and they stepped back as one. Slowly it opened and Selena found herself face to face with the Queen and four nervous-looking guards.

Time slowed down, as Selena's eyes met those of the monarch.

"Well, well, I know you," the slim, rat-faced Queen said slowly, her face cold and a slicer nestling in her arms. "You're Selena Dillon, and you tried to kill me once."

"That's right, and you're lucky it was only the once. I remember it well. Failure isn't something I'm used to, nor is it something I'm particularly proud of."

Behind them reinforcements rushed up the corridor, General Magki amongst them. "Majesty, are you all right?" He demanded, coming to a stop beside Selena and saluting the monarch.

"I'm fine, General, thanks to Captain Dillon and her troops. They saved my life, and I have much to thank them for."

"Well done Dillon," Magki bathed Selena with a smile. Then, eying the carnage around them, he added, "I think we'd better leave you in peace now, Majesty, so your people can clean this mess up."

"Actually I'd rather you came in for a while. You and your men too, Dillon, but leave your weapons by the door. The others can remain outside."

Kes and Braxis followed Selena. They didn't say anything as they handed over their assault rifles and side-arms, though it was obvious none of them were at all happy about it.

"Both of you sit," the Queen began, addressing Selena and the General as the guards took stations around her. Selena's friends stood around protectively, watching the Queen as she sat stroking the weapon laid across her lap. "Firstly, General, I'd be very interested in how the Manta knew to attack my palace. It would appear they might understand our concept of leadership and somehow knew I'd be here. I'd like you to look into that for me, if you will. In the meantime we have a little problem we need to resolve."

Magki looked from the Queen to Selena, and then back again. "We do?"

"Oh yes," she said sitting back, her eyes firmly on Selena, "and you're here as a witness. Now, if I may continue?"

"Please, go ahead," the general answered, worriedly.

"Captain Dillon, may I call you Selena? I know we've had our differences in the past but I want you to know I regret the loss of your parents. As it happens, I knew both of them quite well in the old days. We were all good friends once."

"You expect me to believe that crap?" Selena snapped, leaping to her feet. "Everyone knows you stole my father and then annulled my parents' marriage, before forcing him to marry you."

"Oh, yes," the Queen agreed, solemnly, before shrugging. "I did and for what's it's worth I regret it, but then you know what royalty are like. However, what I've said is true. Your parents, Aunt May and I were all friends a long time ago. If you don't believe me, then look here." she raised her right hand, palm up with a small device in it and a hologram appeared in the air just above it. Selena's throat constricted as she saw an old recording of her mother, father, Aunt May and the Queen laughing together. Then it changed, to show the Queen and her father embracing, then again to one where they were sharing a long and passionate kiss.

"Those are fake," Selena snarled, clenching her fists. "Don't even go there, because I'll cut your goddamn eyes out, and then I'll start to make you really suffer. Killing you is my life's ambition and one day, sooner or later, I'm going to take a great deal of pleasure in doing exactly that."

"Captain, erm, time to go I think..." Singh said, and took Selena firmly by the elbow.

With a last glare at the monarch Selena allowed herself to be led out of the room, while the Queen's voice followed them into the corridor.

"I didn't expect you to believe me, but your Aunt May knows the truth. Ask her, and watch her eyes when she replies."

Then they were outside the building, Selena's breath shuddering as she fought back her rage. She was close to losing control and knew it. Pulling herself together she raised an eyebrow at Braxis and calmed down. He'd collected her weapons and seemed intent on holding on to them.

"What?" she asked.

"Jesus, Captain. You don't do things by half. Remind me not to piss you off."

"Braxis," she growled, striding off, "you haven't seen anything yet."

Chapter Five

Singh and the others escorted her all the way back to the arena, watching silently as she entered her tent. A few moments later she came out to throw a couple of things into the back of a skimmer.

"Are you okay, Ma'am?" Kes asked, glancing from her to Singh.

"I'm fine. Kes, get everyone ready to move out in the morning. Singh, you're coming with me, there's someone I need to see."

Forty minutes later Singh parked the skimmer in a portion of Capulet City reserved as a park. He waited patiently on what passed for a road, while Selena took off her earpiece and walked up the path to the front door of her aunt's old dome-shaped colonial home. She hesitated for just a moment, looking over the well-trimmed lawn and copious multi-coloured flowers in the borders next to the white picket-fenced garden. The buildings had been designed long ago to remind the early settlers of ancient Earth and they brought back warm childhood memories for Selena. She shrugged them aside and knocked loudly.

No answer. She knocked again.

"She's gone away. Left a long time ago," said a voice from behind her.

Selena turned to see a thin, grey haired old woman standing by the garden gate. A light-blue dress hung from her withered frame and she supported herself by leaning on a walking stick.

"Who are you?" Selena asked.

"Oh, don't mind me I'm just a neighbour. I've been tending May's garden while she's away."

"Do you know where she went, or if she'll be back?"

The old woman shook her head, semi-shuffling back and forth. "I've no idea, sorry. She left a long time ago. You'll be Selena. May spoke about you a lot and I remember you as a child, though I doubt you'll remember me. Sorry I can't be of any more help."

Selena bit her lips and then blew out harshly through them. "You can reach me at any time. Just look my name up on the local call-list, or you can contact me via the Penal Corps. Please, let me know if she comes back."

The woman smiled kindly and nodded, watching as Selena got back in the skimmer.

"Not in?" Singh asked.

"No," she replied, looking at him sideways. "I was going to ask my aunt about what the Queen said, but she's gone away. Guess I'll have to wait."

The craft rose and arrowed back towards the arena. It didn't take long but as they were approaching gunfire erupted in the city yet again.

"This is Captain Dillon, what's going on?" she asked over the battlenet, while peering down at the streets through her binoculars.

A woman's voice answered instantly. "We're under attack. We thought we'd killed them all but as we were cleaning up the dead bodies the Manta hit us again. The bugs caught us off guard a second time and we're losing people."

Then she heard Kes say: "Captain, it's Staff Sergeant Philips. They used a typical human tactic, letting us leave cover and then springing an ambush. They made mincemeat of us. We're getting it under control again but it's costing us dear."

"Okay, chuck some anti-personnel mines down those holes and seal them. Treble all guards and I want sonic sensors monitoring those tunnels, and anywhere else that they might pop up. Let's not get caught on the hop a third time."

Once they were landed Selena hurried to Kes's location. He and the others were still sealing the tunnels.

"Anything?" she asked.

"Nope, looks like we got them all. What a mess, but at least we've got the extra sentries posted now and the sonics will help. I've told the others to get back to the camp and get some rest. It's going to be a long day tomorrow."

"Aye," Selena replied. "With a little bit of luck, it'll soon be payback time."

"Are you all right?" Kes asked. "You look a little peaky."

"Just had a bit of a shock, but don't worry it's nothing for you to worry about. With luck all this trouble will stop once we've dealt with the nest tomorrow."

Kes watched her for a moment. "Is it anything I can help with?"

"Oh, no," Selena replied with a shark-like grin, her eyes devoid of all humour. "Just a something I need to catch up on."

"I know you, Selena," he replied, "and that expression. Someone has a whole world of pain coming to them, and I'm sure glad it's not me."

Chapter Six

The forest close to the last Manta nest was dense, which meant rather than set the skimmers on the ground safely a few miles away the troops used their antigravs to float down, watching as the craft disappeared into the morning mist and they themselves into the foliage. Weaving between the trees with the antigravs was slow business but much faster and safer than running or taking the skimmers. Selena, Kes and the others met up with the senior officers in about a quarter of a mile and were there well in time for the General's briefing

"I'm glad you could finally make it, Dillon," General Magki said, "and now that we're all here, I can begin. As you all know, Capulet City was attacked twice last night. Captain Dillon here has suggested the attacks might have been a diversion to take our attention away from the nest. A full recon this morning proves she was right." He turned to the hologram screen hovering in mid-air besides him, and pointed with a glow stick. "Here you can see tracks from the enemy base leading out into the forest. From what we can tell those tracks were made at around the same time the attacks took place.

"The fact they left on foot suggests two things. One they have no craft left, or they know any ships they did have would be blown out of the sky immediately. We have total air and system superiority at this moment in time. Thankfully the attack on Mantis destroyed most of their fleet and we've since found a lot of their other ships dead in space, their crews apparently starved to death. This suggests they haven't been able to rebuild their fleet as yet, which for us is a good thing."

A tall, well-built, tough looking regular officer raised his arm, "You say 'as yet', Sir. Does that mean you're expecting them to do so quickly?"

"Not if we can destroy this base, and then what others they may have. But if they've already been harvesting then yes we can expect them to rebuild fairly quickly. The trouble is we don't know what their industrial capacity is. As to where the bugs from this base have gone, or why, we have no idea. It may be they have another facility we don't know about, or it could be another reason entirely. Whatever it is, we have to track them down and eliminate them. Captain Dillon?"

"Yes Sir?"

"That's your job. You're to take the remains of your century and the seventh, plus replacements, that'll give you two hundred men to work with. Once you know where they're going you either destroy what you find or you call for backup. Got me?"

"Aye, Sir,"

"Major Kramer," the general turned to the officer who'd raised his arm, "that enemy nest still needs to be dealt with. I want you and your regulars to sterilise it."

Selena looked Kramer over. She knew instinctively the general had given him the main mission because the regulars lost face from their failed attack, and he wanted to give them the opportunity to reclaim it. That's exactly what she would have done too, if she were in his place.

"The second section of the Penal Corps will be held back in reserve, just in case either Captain Dillon or Major Kramer runs into trouble," he continued. He minimised the glow stick, turned it off and popped it into a breast pocket. The hologram disappeared moments later. "That's it for now, good luck to you all."

*****

Selena took her time reading through her orders, then she briefed the men and ensured the eight skimmers they'd been assigned formed a line immediately behind each other. Singh and Arthur were to lead in the first craft, with her and Kes in the second while Braxis brought up the

~ 80 ~

rear. At her command the skimmers lifted and set off, following the tracks of the enemy through the trees. As they did so a small object dropped away from the lead craft. It stopped and hovered just about the ground, and then slowly moved ahead of them.

"Arthur, what was that?" Selena asked.

"A bee, I thought it would be a good idea if we used it as a tracker," he replied, "just in case. It should be able to follow them in the dark, and any mist or fog too."

"Good plan. Okay, let's go."

*****

About an hour after they'd set off there was a blinding flash behind them, followed by an ominous rumble as a dark cloud of smoke rose rapidly from the direction of the nest.

Selena immediately called a halt and the craft hovered a few feet above the ground. She tried to contact the general but finally gave up and said, "Nothing from the nest, I can't raise them at all. Hang on..." She listened for a moment, touching her earpiece. Then she blanched and pursed her lips, breathing out through them noisily. "The enemy booby-trapped the last nest! All the troops there, command included, are gone. So apart from those back in the city, we're all that's left." She touched the earpiece again, listened and then added. "Thankfully the general left Colonel Matthews in charge and was on his way back to the city. His skimmer's gone down but there's a rescue team on the way."

"Orders, Ma'am?" Kes asked, loudly, looking straight at her.

"We carry on with the mission, of course. Now at least we don't need to worry about any Manta from the nest sneaking up on us, or the FOM regulars stabbing us in the back. We carry on, find out where these bugs are going and mince them. Capulet City has enough troops to defend

~ 81 ~

itself in the meantime, and there are a lot less bad guys to worry about now."

*****

"These trees are getting thicker," Singh reported. "Even with the tracker we're going to need boots on the ground."

"Arthur," Selena began. "Have you any idea where the enemy might be going?"

"Not a clue, Ma'am, although I'd suggest they're not just running. They're going somewhere fast, so they are working to a plan."

Fourteen hours later Selena called a halt. "That's it for today, let's find a spot and take a breather."

"Are you sure about this?" Kes asked quietly. "The General won't be happy."

"He's probably in hospital and won't be in a position to give a shit. The men need a proper rest, they're exhausted and tired men make mistakes."

With four skimmers hovering protectively over them in a square, the rest of the vehicles settled into a corral. While guards manned the weapons on each skimmer Selena made sure the men were fed, watered and then got some sleep. After inspecting the vehicles she had some of the fragrant casserole a kind soul made up for them all, then climbed into her sleeping bag laid on the grass and under the open sky. Staring at the familiar stars from her childhood she was soon fast asleep.

*****

Selena was awoken by an insane yelping, which turned to a deafening banshee scream. Fighting her way out of the sleeping bag Selena snatched up her machine gun, just as long knee-high dark shapes leapt over the skimmers and ploughed into the stirring men.

"Swords!" Selena shouted, dropping her gun as she grabbed the Katana from the ground next to her sleeping bag. The long blade swept into the night and glinted in the

~ 82 ~

light of the twin moons. The last thing she needed was her men firing blindly into their own ranks. A dark shape before her raised itself as if out of nowhere and stretched towards her face. The creature stood on rear and middle legs, a set of paws from a third and front set reached for her as it opened its jaws, revealing shark-like teeth dribbling with pendulous strings of gluey saliva. Jumping to her right Selena swung the mighty blade in a hissing arc down to her left. It connected with a solid thunk and then slipped through whatever she'd hit. There was a gibbering scream as something monstrous dropped to the grass, where it scrabbled insanely for a moment and then stilled.

"Lights!" she bellowed skipping backwards, her eyes dancing in all directions with her sword held ready in both hands. As the hovering skimmers illuminated the whole area Selena bulked, it couldn't be…Creatures that resembled a cross between some form of long, hip-high six-legged rabid dog and a very wide cat blinked black eyes that were almost lost in short dark fur at the sudden light, then they turned tail and ran, bounding easily over the circle of skimmers and sank back into the night-cloaked forest.

"If anyone has an idea what those were," Kes gasped. "I'd like to know. I've never seen anything like that before"

"Monsters from the past," Selena replied, shuddering and still unable to believe her eyes. "They're lenars."

"Jesus, that's all we need," Kes said, eying the one Selena had cut clean in half.

Selena wiped her blade and looked at him. "When the colonists first came here these things tore them to pieces. We knew nothing about them initially, because they have a low heat signature and so weren't picked up by thermal imaging. They sleep during the day, digging deep into the ground and covering themselves when the sun rises, and so the flybys didn't spot them. They diurnal, but prefer to hunt in the dark."

Selena told them about the unfortunate first explorers who had decided to camp right on top of a whole pack of them. She remembered being told at school that all the others found was blood, pieces of bone and their equipment. She was silent for a moment, then added, "That's why Capulet City's perimeter defence was kept, to defend us against them, while other worlds that didn't face such threats soon changed the standard base design."

"So how come we weren't warned about them?" Braxis asked, looking about nervously

"Because we thought we'd killed them all off," Selena replied. "No one's seen them for centuries."

"Christ, their blood stinks," Braxis observed, one hand holding his nose.

"Yeah, as I recall it's something to do with a defensive mechanism." Selena shuddered again, as she cleaned her blade. "Not that I can imagine them having any enemies for long. When we were at school we were taught they usually attack in packs, but they'll also fight to the death on their own if they're cornered."

"Great, what else do we know about them?" Singh asked.

"They're clever, and were known to sneak into houses at night," Selena replied. "They took people from their beds so silently the others in the house could be sleeping right next to them and yet they wouldn't hear a thing. The first anyone knew about it was when they woke up next to blood-soaked bedding. Countless times the lenars dragged young children from their cots then yammered outside, waking the rest of the household. When the distraught parents ran out to look for their children, they ran smack into packs of them. Nobody could figure out why they only took one person at a time, although some speculated it was a damn effective terror tactic. It's also why there were no dogs on Capulet for a long time. The lenars liked eating them. In fact they specifically went for houses that had them, so dogs came to be seen as bad luck. A fair few have been imported since, but even so..."

"That suggests a high intelligence," Arthur said, cleaning his machine gun, hand weapon drawn and by his side.

"Oh, like I said they're clever. Our people became so terrified of them they even poisoned their farm animals and let them loose in the forests outside the city, in the hope the lenars would go for them. The settlers would rather have starved than meet a horrific death at the jaws of those monsters. It worked too. The lenars died in their thousands, although several were still killed by the perimeter defence over the following years. They caught on quickly, but it was too late the poisons decimated them. Their raids and numbers gradually ceased and we finally hoped we'd killed them all.

"They've not been seen for centuries, although there was always a chance that a few might still exist somewhere." Selena shook her head to clear it of the horror. "But, for them to be this close to the city?"

Several troops collected the lenars' carcases and dumped them a short distance away, playing their beam weapons over the bodies until they were reduced to ashes, but still that harsh hot metallic smell lingered.

"A word?" Kes asked, sidling up to her and handing over a cup of hot coffee.

"Sure, Kes, what is it?"

"Something's been bothering me." He took a sip of the beverage and blew gently at the steaming surface.

The scent of hot coffee reached Selena, stomach grumbling, and she took a sip of her own drink. "Like I said, what is it?"

"Apart from shortly after the reinforcements arrived the Manta haven't attacked us, why not?"

"Perhaps they were conserving or building up their numbers."

"That's exactly my point if you think about it. We know they had the numbers. There were thousands of them at the nest we attacked, remember? When we assaulted it they just swarmed out and came at us in waves so thick you couldn't even count them. On top of that they obviously knew how to get into Capulet, yet they didn't until they had no choice."

Selena frowned. "You're right, that doesn't make sense. They only attacked when they needed to divert our attention, when they made their escape."

"So, we're missing something, and whatever it is I've a feeling it's really important." Kes said, reaching out to touch her arm. "Are you okay? You look a little peaky."

Selena pulled her arm back and quickly stepped away, looking at him in confusion. "I'm fine, but what are you doing?"

"Sorry, I didn't mean anything by it."

She watched his face go beetroot for a moment and then shrugged it off. "Forget it. There's something else I need to talk to you about. Kes, it's insights like this that's made me recommend you for promotion. You're wasted as an NCO."

"Say what?" Now it was Kes's turn to be surprised. "I've already been promoted, I'm a Staff Sergeant, remember?"

"You're bumped to Lieutenant, with immediate effect. I spoke to the Admiral about it before we left and I received confirmation from him this morning, hence why I made us a little late for the general's briefing. When all this is over you're going back to Hades Prime, for Officer Training."

"With respect Ma'am, you can shove that. I'm not going back to that hellhole where we did our basic training. Selena, I still have nightmares about it. The answer is no."

"You think I'm giving you a choice, Kes? This is the Penal Regiments. Our numbers are depleted and we badly need men like you to replace the officers we've lost. So tough shit, it's a done deal. When you complete the training you'll have a command of your own. I'll miss your ugly screwed up mug, not to mention the awful ginger hair; but that's the end of the matter." She paused. "What is it, Singh?"

He saluted and handed her a message tablet. She looked at the small screen. "Damn."

"Something important?" Kes asked.

"Just confirmation that Kramer and his men, plus our other section and the colonel, are all dead. The whole area is nothing but ashes. The general's ordered us to carry on with the mission, as I thought he would." She handed the tablet back to Singh. "Tell the men we move out at daybreak."

*****

None of them slept well for the rest of the night. The lenars slunk through the trees just outside the light, their growling and gibbering rose and fell, turning to sudden eldritch screams which caused everyone to scrabble for their weapons and take up defensive positions. As daylight came the lenars finally fell silent and the troops were beyond exhausted.

"Do you think the Manta have had any trouble with those things?" Singh asked, as the seniors met for a briefing before moving on.

"Let's hope so," Kes replied. "Captain, the men are tired, they didn't get much sleep. I'd like to suggest they take turns sleeping on the skimmers while we travel, with guards posted on each side of the craft."

"Good idea," Selena agreed. "I want all meals cooked on board during their rest periods. That way everyone gets fed without disturbance. Arthur, anything you can do about the lenars?"

"Not at the moment, but believe me when I say I'm thinking about it."

"Think faster."

That evening they came across a battle scene showing the Manta had indeed fallen foul of the lenars. A scorched and trampled area of the forest was filled with dead Manta and lenars. Selena ordered four skimmers to land while she investigated.

"Jesus, what a smell," Arthur observed, kicking one of the dead lenars which had its jaws locked around a Manta limb.

"By the look of it, Ma'am, your local nasties came unstuck," Singh observed." The Manta took them apart, although it cost them dearly by the look of it. How many do you think the Manta lost?"

"Hard to say," Selena replied, glancing at the alien bodies. "At least fifty or so, but that's not nearly as many as the lenars."

"Well, it's fifty less for us to kill," Singh replied. Boarding his skimmer he waited for Selena and then they all moved on.

The trees grew taller as their journey progressed. Arthur reported his bee had gone missing so, despite her misgivings, Selena had no choice but to order the skimmers to drop below the tree-line. She knew full well they daren't lose sight of their target's tracks in the vehicles lights.

Selena tried to keep them going through the night, their transport's lights and cameras picking up the tracks, but several times the lenars leapt from branches directly into the skimmers, creating chaos and death. Eventually she bought them to a halt and called her officers and NCO's together.

"Enough," she said. "They've caught on. They know we have to fly below the branches. We're going to need a strong force on the ground, with the skimmers providing covering fire from above. I know it's not ideal but unfortunately I don't see us having any other choice, we can't risk the transport."

"The men aren't going to be happy," Singh replied.

"The Captain's right," Kes interjected. "We're fighting them on their terms. We either fly above the trees, where they can't get at us yet miss seeing the Manta if they go into hiding, or we have a large force on the ground that's sufficient to deal with them while the skimmers provide air cover. It's a long walk home guys, so we need to look after the skimmers."

"Okay," Selena said, "I want a pilot and four in each skimmer, plus any wounded and those resting. Six hours each stint, those on board cook the meals for each crew. Everyone else walks, and eats during their rest period."

An hour later the lenars struck again, but as they leapt from the trees they were met with a hail of fire that tore them to shreds. Not one soldier was injured and Selena noticed a dramatic improvement in morale. "See, I told you they were pussy cats," she murmured, with a smile.

It was sunset when the ground erupted in front of the troops, the lenars boiling into their midst. Instantly the troops formed a solid defensive ring around them, those on the inside using their swords on any of the creatures within the circle, while the troops on the outside used their heavier weapons on the creatures that leapt from the trees or raced over the ground towards them. More and more lenars came, yet not one reached their ranks. The skimmers overhead joined the battle, beam and projectile weapons smashing through the foliage. The fighting went on and on. More of the creatures slunk out of the shadows and raced towards them, lips drawn back to reveal slavering jaws. Then quite suddenly it was all over, and an eerie quiet filled the forest.

"Christ, we must have killed hundreds of the beggars," Kes said.

"How many troops have we lost?" Selena asked.

"We've only a few wounded. We weren't taken by surprise this time. It could have been a lot worse," he replied.

She watched as the troops started to shoot the wounded lenars, when someone shouted, "Just cut their paws off and let them die. Hopefully it'll put the others off."

"Belay that," she snapped. "Give them a quick death. No creature deserves to suffer needlessly."

The skimmers landed and the wounded were put aboard, and a short while later they were on their way again.

"There's a large clearing ahead," Singh informed Selena three hours later, from overhead.

"Thanks, we'll rest there and get a hot brew going," she replied with relief.

Three skimmers remained aloft, while the remaining craft grounded and formed about them defensively. They'd barely settled when a cacophony of shrieking came the undergrowth and more lenars raced like greyhounds towards them, but by now the troops were used to them and were ready. Side-by-side they stood and hosed fire into the oncoming creatures, killing dozens. Overhead the skimmers were adding their fire to the carnage when suddenly, from the far side of the clearing, fire from an unknown source laced into the creatures. Caught in such crossfire the lenars stood little chance. Shortly after, the battle was over.

"Kes, come with me," Selena ordered, and set off at a brisk walk towards the far side of the clearing, where their supporting fire had come from. She stopped dead in her tracks, as shadows moved in the gloom between the trees. Together they peered into the forest.

"Fuck," Kes yelled suddenly, raising his weapon.

"Hold!" Selena bellowed, slapping his weapon down towards the ground.

The Manta stood in front of them, unmoving, their weapons down by their sides. Man and alien stood silently, watching and waiting for the other to make a move.

Chapter Seven

The silence stretched, and the dark greens of the foliage grew lighter as the sunrise turned the sky a cherry red. The strong earthy smell of the forest somehow became richer and far more acute, and Selena swallowed as she gazed at the enemy who stood still, staring straight back at her with those vermillion eyes – the top two, mechanical, moving independently of the others.

Both sides remained still.

"Nobody move," Selena said softly, into the battlenet. "There's to be no firing, unless I say so."

An orange glowing metallic ball appeared over the right shoulder of the lead creature, and a voice beyond description said, "We were mistaken yet don't understand. The makeup of your bodies is that of our old enemy, the Cetra. You're the same, but not. It was only when we captured your vessels and accessed your information we realised our error. We've been watching you. How is it you are them, and yet not them?"

"What are they on about?" Kes growled. "Let's just kill the fuckers and be done with it."

"Shhh, she hissed. Then answered loudly, "We call them the ForeRunners. It's possible they were our ancestors, although we've never even met them. All we've found are their ruins all over the galaxy."

The glowing orb swirled. "You are the same, but not."

"We have nothing to do with them. We defended ourselves because you attacked us."

"You, the ancient enemy, stained our worlds. The Cetra, your ForeRunners, are to be erased."

"We aren't them," Selena insisted.

There was silence for a moment, and then the Manta spoke again. "Yesssssss. We will go, soon."

"Go where?" Selena asked.

"Away. Those that were coming for us were destroyed. We've called on…friends."

"What do you mean, 'friends'?" Kes asked, with a frown.

"Captain," Singh's voice demanded through her earpiece. "I know you're kinda busy right now, and I wouldn't usually interrupt, but something's coming."

Selena touched her earpiece. "What do you mean, 'something'?"

"Exactly that, Ma'am, I haven't got a bloody clue what it is. I can't make it out. But it's big, damn big, and will be here shortly, it's travelling incredibly fast."

"This war is a waste of lives," Selena shouted to the Manta. Squinting, she couldn't even make out the silver insignia on the criss-cross webbing that she knew would be there. All she could see was their spider-mantis shapes swaying back and forth in the shadows of the trees. "Is there a way we can stop it?"

"Perhaps," the creature replied. "We go now."

Overhead a large gelatinous orb of constantly changing colour swept into sight and stopped instantly. It was so large it blotted out the sky above them and cast a huge shadow over the forest. A small section began to bulge from the side. Detaching itself it floated down towards them, settling gently in the grass on Selena's left, between them and the Manta. Despite its size there was no noise at all. As soon as it touched down the Manta began scrambling from the forest and running directly into the rainbow skin, simply disappearing within as if they had dived into water. The Manta with the orange orb, however, remained exactly where it was.

"What is that?" Selena demanded, pointing her left hand at the craft.

"Allies. They did not take part in the war against you and the…ForeRunners, but they have come to help us leave this place."

~ 93 ~

Just then a creature detached itself from the strange craft and drifted towards them.

"Good grief," Kes gasped, "that's one of those weird things from Arcadia. Remember the one that sat on the branch and got scoffed by the tree?"

"You have a way with words...But, yeah, you're right."

The creature hovered in the air in front of them. Its many eyes, if you could call them that, were round black tips at the end of long writhing stalks. The creature itself looked like a jellified seahorse, this one translucent and blue. It stared at the humans for a while, its stalks squirming in different directions like snakes.

"We have to go now," the Manta said and lumbered towards the strange vessel on the ground. "Your ships are coming."

Just then three small patrol craft shot over the horizon and opened fire with canons at the alien craft, which although hit repeatedly remained undamaged. The armour piercing, explosive shells had no effect at all. It was like dropping pebbles into water, they were simply swallowed up. Instantly globs of matter flew from the craft towards one of the human ships and hit it. The patrol ship wobbled and limped away, trailing smoke. The other two ships swung back in a tight circle and attacked again, this time with beam weapons. As the rays struck there was a sizzling sound and cuts appeared in the craft's skin, but these resealed instantly. This time the alien ship fired a multitude of black globs at both craft. The projectiles hit, and then encompassed the human vessels. Split seconds later the stains on the patrol craft turned black and fell away like dust, taking most of the vessels' structure with it. Spinning out of control the remains of the two ships crashed into the forest and exploded, smoke rising over the trees.

"That ship just took out three of ours," "Braxis said over the battlenet, "we've got to do something!"

"Like what?" Selena asked. "Those regular ships had far superior weapons than we have, and they didn't even make a dent in it. Plus we're pretty exposed here. Besides, those weren't our ships, they were the Federations and no doubt that's less for us to face later on. Nobody does anything, unless I say so."

"Look, there's more Manta," Kes pointed with his right index finger towards the dark depths of the forest.

He was right. Long streams of the enemy emerged from the trees and lopped towards the alien craft. Each of them carried something in their arms and suddenly Selena realised what it was. "Chrysalides," she gasped. "They're carrying chrysalides!"

"If any of those are Queens then humanity's had it, they'll breed like wildfire and you know it. We have to destroy them," Arthur growled, approaching Selena from behind.

The Manta with the Orb over its shoulder swivelled its eyes towards Arthur, as he walked purposefully towards them. Instantly its demeanour changed. The Manta snapped its weapon upright but even as it did so Selena's machine gun hammered explosive shells into it, cutting the creature in half. Instantly her team followed her lead. Beams, and bullets raked the aliens, and grenades burst amidst those carrying the chrysalides. Manta and foliage were blown to pieces, torn to shreds and thrown aside as if by an angry god. As one of the Manta carrying an egg leapt desperately at the alien craft Selena snapped four rounds after it, and saw part of the left side of the creature's fly away. Even as the strange craft swallowed the Manta it was already falling, the burden dropping from its arms. The amoebic vessels outer skin closed up after them, as they fell through.

Within moments not one Manta remained standing. The silence after the hellish cacophony was unbelievable, and Selena turned to find herself face to face with the seahorse-like creature from the strange craft. Somehow she read disbelief and sorrow emanating from the creature. It watched her for a moment or two and then turned away, drifting as if on an unfelt wind toward the blob-like craft on the ground. It simply vanished into the side of the craft. No doors opened, no hatchway materialised, it just melted into the side of the ship. Then the blob rose silently from the ground and, gaining speed, joined the bulky rainbow craft high overhead, like a raindrop joining a puddle. The vast craft rotated several times then shot skywards. Faster and faster it went, until it had disappeared into the heavens.

Her men advanced towards the tree line and gunshots rang out, as they came across wounded Manta. She watched as they fired into the chrysalides, pulping them, gore splashing their uniforms. At length silence reigned once more. Between the dead lenars on one side and the Manta on another, it was like standing in the middle of a charnel house.

"On me, now."

When her friends stood beside her Selena turned to Arthur, her eyes burning like lasers. "Lower that weapon. Singh, take it away from him. What happened here, Arthur, and why did that Manta lose the plot when you appeared? You'd better explain yourself, and fast."

Arthur surrendered his weapon and held his hands open in front of his chest. "Hey, I'm as surprised as you are. I've no idea what happened, but I'm right in what I said and you know it."

Selena pulled her knife free and walked up to him, pressing the point under his chin, forcing him to lift his head and raise his eyes to meet hers. "You lying son of a bitch. They helped us when we were being attacked and they had no need to. We actually had a chance of ending this war and then you come along and it all goes to rat shit. Bit of a coincidence, wouldn't you say?"

Arthur met the cold fury in her eyes quite calmly. "The fact they talked to us means they could have done so at any time. They said they only realised their error when they captured our ships, yet they got hold of the Lexington and her crew when she was on trials and that was a long time ago. We saw her during our mission to attack Mantis, if you remember. Think about it, they only helped us so we would allow them to escape but we couldn't do that and you know it. They'd only breed and attack us again. Oh, and when you asked if there could be peace between us they didn't exactly reach out, shake hands and say 'oh yeah, sure, that'll be nice.' They said 'perhaps'. Not exactly promising, was it."

"So, why did they behave as they did when they saw you?"

"I don't know," Arthur replied, exasperated. "Maybe it's because I'm just plain ugly. Look at me. I was repaired by the ForeRunner technology. I may look normal to you but perhaps they saw me as some kind of threat."

"Yeah, well I can certainly see their point," Selena replied, putting her knife back in its sheath before pushing him away roughly with both hands, then stepping up close until she was an inch or two from him face. "I don't trust you, Arthur. You've changed. There's something about you that isn't right."

Arthur's eyes bore into hers. "Are you going to say that to Hope too, and her parents? There's nothing different between her and I. Both of us have been altered by the ForeRunners, it doesn't make us bad guys. You really need to rethink who your friends and enemies are. Those things have killed billions of us, what the hell have Hope or I done? Oh, and tell me, would you hold a knife up to Hope's throat? I've fought alongside you, Selena, when we had little or no hope of survival. I was even killed right next to you, not that I remember it, and yet you treat me like this."

He stepped back, turned and stalked away.

Selena watched him without a word, then the general's voice came over the battlenet.

"Captain Dillon, give me a situation report. We've just had two patrol craft shot down and another damaged by an unknown vessel in your area."

"That craft was acting in self-defence, Sir. Our ships opened fire on it without provocation. I've no idea what kind of ship it was but it's nothing we've seen before and belonged to an unknown party, which I'll tell you about when I see you. It retaliated initially with warning shots and damaged one of our craft. The other two didn't take the hint and came back for another go. You can understand why it took them out."

"Roger. What's the situation now?"

Selena spoke quickly, eager to get on with the mission. "The alien ship came to rescue the Manta, but we killed them and the craft has left now. I'd like my team to continue a bit further if that's okay, Sir. I can't see the enemy would come all this way just to meet an alien craft, when they could have defended their position and been picked up there. I want to make sure we're not missing anything."

"Okay, it makes sense. But I want to see you in my office when you get back. You and I need to talk."

"Aye, Sir," she replied, "I'll keep you updated. Dillon, out."

Selena ordered a breather. Her troops were tired and restless, and so was she. From practice the military could sleep anywhere, any time, but when they weren't sleeping — even during their breaks — they were constantly alert and searching for trouble, inevitably it wore you down.

An hour or so later it began to rain. It was gentle at first, then the sky exploded into a torrent of thick droplets, whipped about by a fierce wind that blew the water sideways. She extended the break, it was pointless going on in this weather. A light repeller field above them kept them relatively sheltered from above, while they donned light foul-weather gear against the slashing sideways onslaught. As soldiers do, they pulled their clothing around them and made the best of it, waiting out the storm while one of them aboard each craft cooked the rest of his crew a meal. The aromatic smell of the dark-brown stew, filled with bright-red carrots, potatoes, turnips, other locally grown vegetables and mutton from the local farming community was torn away by the gale but just the thought of it made Selena's mouth water. Luckily each craft had a silver-coloured foldaway hob at the back with a pull-over cover, on which they cooked group meals from basic materials when they weren't using self-heating packs. The instant on-off heat dissipated in no time at all, which meant the equipment could be folded away in under a minute in case of emergency.

Kes bought Selena her a good portion of the stew, plus a hunk of granary bread, and hunkered down beside her with his own meal.

"Thanks," she dug in with a spoon and savoured the taste. "This is one of my favourite meals. It reminds me of what Aunt May often cooked."

"I'm glad we brought some fresh supplies and thought you must like it, I saw your nose twitching from five feet away."

She looked at him sideways and took another mouthful. "Well, I'm sure this is much better for us than the processed crap we usually get."

"I've been looking at the maps," he replied. "This forest ends before long, then the moors begin. So, if something is here we should find it pretty shortly. I do believe the rain's finally easing off."

"Can you hear that?" Selena asked, her head cocked to her left, listening.

"What?"

"Listen."

Kes did so and caught his breath. "You mean that sound, like a puppy whimpering? No idea, but I'll be rogered sideways if you think I'm going out there to find out." He looked pointedly into the night. "You can't see more than a few feet, and what little you can looks pretty damn muddy and treacherous."

"Well," Selena replied her bottom lip curling, "you stay here if you like but I'm not going to ignore it." Putting down her dinner she leapt over the side of the craft into the downpour. In the middle of a curse, Kes picked up his weapon, cocked it and followed her.

He caught up quickly and side by side they squelched past the tattered and torn trees, the grey ashes of their adversaries in the burnt ground long since washed away. Then Selena stopped, holding up a hand at the sudden silence. She cut away sharply to the left and into the thick green rubbery undergrowth. Within moments they were gazing down at the body of a female lenar, its offspring lying dead beside it in the mire. Then a slight movement caught Selena's eye. One of them was still alive.

Kes aimed his weapon, only to have Selena knock it aside.

"What are you doing?" she asked.

"It can't survive without its mother, best to put it out of misery."

"No way," Selena reached down and moved the mother's body aside, picking the cub up from underneath her by the scruff of its neck. No longer than half her forearm the creature twisted and turned, trying to bite her with razor-like teeth. Selena tapped it sharply across the nose with the tips of her fingers. "No," she said firmly. As it looked up at her, Selena felt oddly drawn to the creature and swiftly tucked the squirming bundle of fur under her right arm, where it calmed down.

Kes never said a word as they marched back through the downpour and vaulted over the side of their skimmer but Singh took one look and stepped back, saying:

"You have got to be shitting me..."

"Its parents are dead and it's been left all alone," Selena said. "I've been there myself, so I know how it feels."

Selena sat and put her mess tin on the floor. Grabbing the lenar pup she held it out straight in front of her and then stared into the black almond-shaped eyes blending so perfectly into the thick matching fur. The creature growled ominously, squirmed and raised its hackles, the claws on all six feet flexing. In the gloom of the rainy night it was a dark, shadowy lump in her hands.

"Dinner," she said, putting the creature on the floor and ushering it towards the food.

The lenars button nose twitched. Its eyes swivelled towards the meal, then back and forth between Selena and her offering. Tentatively it moved towards the tray, sniffed and licked at the rapidly congealing mess of food and rain with a long grey tongue. Then it began to feed. It ate the lot and when it was finished the lenar sat back and looked up at Selena. It was no longer growling.

As she reached to pick it up the creature snapped at her hand yet again. Instantly she responded by tapping it again across the nose, then did so a second time. "No," she said again, firmly, while wagging a warning finger. When she tried to pick it up again the creature didn't object. She stroked its back and ticked it under the chin. Turning to face the disbelieving looks of her team she said:

"Hey, meet Shadow. I always wanted a pet."

*****

The rain stopped finally and a short while later they set off. Before long they came across a building of Manta design. It stood alone, buried deep in the forest, surrounded and overshadowed by trees. It was one of the emerald-coloured rectangular structures, sat balanced insanely on one corner. From the corner of her eye Selena saw many of her comrades lean their heads to one side, as if for a better view or to try and make some sense of it.

As the skimmers landed Selena leapt out. "Kes, Select ten men and come with me. Singh, Arthur, you're with me too. The rest of you move back to a safe place and cover us if you can, just in case they've booby trapped it, and take those skimmers with you."

Cautiously Selena and the others entered the building. Bottle-green light shone through the sides of the building, giving everything an eerie glow. Looking around them they saw the building was basically just a shell, with half-finished girders above them on which the beginnings of other floors lay.

"Hmm," Arthur began, "By the look of it I'd say this was the start of another nest. One they didn't get the chance to complete."

"There are chrysalides on the floor over there," Braxis said, pointing to their left.

"You men, guard those," Selena ordered. "If any Manta appear, destroy the eggs first. The rest of you explore the other floors, and be careful." She watched as some of them activated their gravpacks and floated up through the girders while others disappeared into the gloom ahead on foot. She was updating the general when they all came back, a few minutes later.

"There's nothing here, Ma'am," Singh reported. "Looks like Arthur could be right about it being the start of a nest." He nodded towards the mound by her feet. "Aren't you going to smash those?"

"Nope, I've a feeling the powers that be might want them, and this building, in one piece." She was right. As soon as she told the general, he replied, "Return to the city as soon as you can and bring those things with you. Leave a contingent of troops at the building to guard it. I'll send someone to relieve them as soon as I can."

She called in those she'd held in reserve and, leaving Kes in charge, Selena and the others headed for home.

*****

Magki was pleased to see her, until he saw Shadow nestling in her arms. His smile faded.

"What the hell is that?"

"It's a lenar, Sir, a young one. Couldn't leave it there to die, now could I?"

"I can't make you out, Selena. One moment you're a hardnosed bitch and the next you're adopting something you wouldn't wish on your worst enemy. Anyone would think you had a soft spot." He peered at her more closely. "No, I guess not. Anyway, I wanted to say well done on the mission. That building and the chrysalides are real prizes, intelligence are going to have a field day with them. I take it you checked the structure for booby traps? I'd hate to lose more men in the way we did at the last nest, tragic waste."

"We checked and it's all clear. The thing that concerns me is we attacked an alien craft, which is pretty dumb as it means we've basically declared war on an unknown race. What clown ordered that?"

"I did," a voice said from behind her.

A low rumble issued from Shadow, as Selena turned to face a FOM Regular Forces commander entering through an open side door. Tall and overweight there was something about his grey eyes that made her uneasy, even though his gaze was firm and unflinching. He didn't hold out his hand, as was the norm, instead he stood with his hands clasped behind him, a large and powerful brown dog at his side.

"And you are?" Selena queried.

"I'm Commander Muller," he said.

"Muller?"

"Yes, that's right. You knew my younger brother. He was the base commander on Loreen when you originally got there. Sadly he died in the other ship in your mission, the one that attacked the Manta sun."

Eyes narrowing, Selena considered him for a moment. "Your brother was an asshole, but he died bravely I'll give him that." To her surprise she saw an unfathomable glint in Muller's eyes and a half smile tugging at his lips.

"I was told you were direct, which I admire. My brother and I were estranged over family matters, we hadn't spoken in years. None-the-less I was sorry to hear of his death but at least he died well. As for the alien craft, it was helping the Manta. As such it took sides and was considered an enemy." A low rumble came from his dog as it strained at the leash.

Shadow stirred in her arms and stretched his neck towards Muller, a much deeper rumble sounding in his throat. The dog stopped and backed away. Muller reddened, as Shadow turned its eyes to him. Then he swallowed and stepped back too.

"Not exactly a friendly little begger, is it?" He managed. "I was hoping you and I can be friends, Selena. I'm not my brother."

"No, you're not, but I take it brains don't run in your family. Your brother's attitude to the locals on Loreen led to them siding with the rebels. Yours could lead us into another war, one against an enemy we know nothing about. As far as I'm concerned you're a prime example of what happens when cousins breed. With regard to the dog, apparently lenars developed a taste for them a long time ago, so I'd keep him close by if I were you." She turned to the General. "If you'll excuse me, Sir?"

It was obvious Magki didn't trust himself to speak. He tried hard to hide his smile and simply nodded.

Saluting, Selena strode from the room and shut the door behind her.

*****

Shadow grew rapidly and followed Selena everywhere she went, even to the extent of sleeping on the end of her bed. They developed quite a bond and, oddly, the creature seemed to anticipate her. She found when they were walking he would lead her the way she intended going, even to the extent that if she changed her mind Shadow appeared to know. Selena's notoriety increased rapidly. She stayed out of Muller's way and he out of hers. The months passed quickly but the locals remained understandably wary of shadow and quickly moved out of their way, while watching with wide disbelieving and fearful eyes.

"I'm sorry Ma'am," the guard said, stepping in front of her as she arrived at the officers' mess, a larger than usual tent in the arena, where they'd arranged to meet Kotes during one of his fleeting visits. "You can't bring that thing into the mess."

"This isn't a *thing*, it's a lenar." Selena turned to Shadow. "Go on home," she watched as he turned and headed off to their tent. Entering the mess she saw the others all there before her, with Singh ordering a round of Roget's Revenge. She was just about to speak when someone put a hand on her shoulder, to her surprise Selena turned to find herself face-to-face with Muller.

"Dillon, it's about time you and I had a chat. You embarrassed me in front of the old man. I don't forgive things like that easily. You owe me an apology."

"That was ages ago, Muller. Grow up, life's too short. I tell you what, though. I'll owe you a hand in a moment, so either move it or lose it."

"You may think you're something special, but you're going to pay for that insult."

"You've had too much to drink, Muller. I suggest you go home, while you still can."

His free hand grabbed her throat and squeezed, making it hard for her to breath. Instantly Selena scooped up a swizzle stick from the bar and rammed it under his right eyeball. His scream, as he staggered back with the stick protruding from beneath his eye, brought the place to a standstill.

"I do hope that was the eye you had on me," she murmured calmly. "I suggest if you want to keep the other one, you stay away from me."

Still screaming and cursing Muller was dragged outside and off to sickbay by several of his friends. To her amusement Selena noticed those around her moved away and kept their distance, so although the bar was crowded Selena and her team stood in a space of their own.

"He chose his moment well," Kes offered. "You didn't have Shadow with you. I'd say your lenar scares him."

"Well, he's not alone there, it sure terrifies the shit out of me," Singh added. "Don't you read history books?"

"It's just a baby," she explained. "You wouldn't abandon a human child, now would you?"

He was silent for a moment. "No, I guess not. Drink up, it's Kotes's round next and we all know how rare a treat that is. I won't know whether to drink it, or frame it."

Much later, as they headed back to their tents, Kes asked if he could have a word with her.

"Sure," she replied, as she entered her billet. "Come on in."

As they entered Shadow already knew they were there. He looked from one of them to the other, then lay back down again yet watched them constantly.

"Drink?" Selena asked. When Kes nodded she poured them both a single measure of scotch and handed

~ 106 ~

him his. "What is it?" she asked. As he moved close to her she couldn't help but look into his eyes.

"This officer training you've put me forward for, I don't want it."

"Why not?" she asked with a slight frown.

"You really want to know?"

"Kes, I wouldn't ask otherwise."

"Very well, then let me show you." He leant forward and kissed her gently on the lips. "Sorry, just thought you ought to be aware. Yeah, I know you Miss Bryn. For what it's worth I liked and admired him, he was a good man." He reached up suddenly and ran his fingers over his lips.

"What are you doing?" she asked.

"Just counting them, to make sure they're still there. I guess I'd better go, while I'm one piece."

Selena put her drink down and reached for him. "No, actually, I'd rather you stayed."

*****

Early next morning Selena found herself in front of the general. "You sent for me, Sir?"

He gestured for her to sit down and looked at her sombrely. "You do realise Muller lost that eye last night."

"Rather careless of him, Sir."

"This isn't funny, Dillon. You've made a powerful enemy. I'd watch your back if I were you. Luckily there were witnesses and all of them say he assaulted you, a senior officer. In my book that means he deserved it, so I'm putting this down as self-defence. I mean what I say, though, watch your back."

"Thank you, I'll keep it in mind. Is there anything else?"

"Yes, you're not related to that young woman in the control room are you, Lieutenant Roberts?"

"I don't believe so, why?"

"She reminds me of you and apparently doesn't like Muller either. Word has it he kept getting her to take his dog outside for a sniff and she finally had a sense of humour failure. This morning she fed that hound laxatives before locking the poor thing in Muller's office. It made quite a mess by all accounts. Luckily, he doesn't know it was her but not a lot escapes me."

Selena snorted. "She sounds like my kind of person. What happened to the dog?"

"He's since sold it to palace security. The reason I asked you here is I'm sending a group of scientists out to the Manta building you found. Select a team, escort them and make sure they stay safe."

"When do we leave?"

"In a couple of hours. I want the building examined as soon as possible, before something happens to it. Another thing, orders arrived from Admiral Van Pluy this morning for Kes Phillips to report for officer training. I see him as an essential member of your team but according to these orders he should be on the next transport, which leaves this evening. Do you want me to hold onto him for a while? I'm sure I can wangle it."

"No, Sir. It's all fine with me. I'll let him know right away. Is there anything else?"

"Yes, keep a close eye on your lenar. It's growing quickly. I know you're attached to it, but I just want to play safe."

"I will, Sir." Selena gave a curt nod, saluted and left the room.

Chapter Eight

Selena went straight to Kes's tent to give him the news. She saw the hurt and disbelief in his eyes and said sincerely, "You need this, Kes. You'll make a damn good officer and we both know it. Anyhow, I have to go. A mission's come up. Arthur and Singh are coming with me and we leave in a bit, so we won't be here to say our goodbyes."

"Selena..."

"Your transport leaves tonight at eight. Take good care of yourself." She offered a smile then turned and walked away.

They took three skimmers, herself and Braxis in the first, Arthur in the second and Singh in the last. They split twenty troops and a handful of scientists and engineers between them. Selena was reluctant to take more troops than she needed, and was well aware they could all do with the rest but with luck this would just be a babysitting job. Skimming the treetops they arrived at the site relatively quickly. On landing Selena ordered Arthur to relieve the others who'd been guarding the site and to send them back for some rest. In no time at all they'd vanished into the distance, leaving only Selena and her group. Arthur checked the sentry guns and posted guards, while the remainder set up camp.

"Captain Dillon?"

The man had introduced himself earlier as Cox, the leading scientist of the civilian group. He was a small, rather rotund man with a balding head and jolly expression. He also seemed to sweat a lot, and even now was mopping his brow with a cloth. Her eyes were drawn to the multi-coloured beads adorning his long, mousey-coloured dread-locked beard.

"Yes, what is it?"

"I just wanted to say thanks for escorting us. None of us can think of anyone we'd rather have with us, I know a few of the others are worried about the lenars."

As if by magic Shadow appeared from behind Selena and stopped at her side, staring up at the man intently. He whitened and stepped back, again wiping his brow with the cloth.

"I find them rather intriguing," Selena replied. "In the wild they're killers but, for some reason, Shadow hasn't been a problem."

"I'll take your word for it," Cox replied. "They killed a lot of people over the years, and I know most hoped they were gone for good."

"I'm sure you've got work to do, Mr Cox. Best you get on with it." She watched as he waddled off, imagining the damp footsteps he left in his wake. "Arthur, take two men and look after those scientists, keep an eye on what they're doing while you're at it." Then she selected Braxis and two others and went to inspect the perimeter, leaving Singh in charge.

The sentry guns all checked out and Selena was spending a few moments chatting to the perimeter guards, when suddenly Shadow stiffened besides her. "What is it, boy?" she asked. Following the lenar's gaze she saw a small deer-like creature weaving in and out of the trees. "Ah dinner, go on then."

Instantly Shadow bounded towards the creature, bowling it over it amidst the foliage. Locking its jaws around the creature's throat Shadow quickly killed the animal and began to feed. Selena and her escorts were moving towards Shadow when he stiffened suddenly, then silently rose to his feet.

Selena held up a hand. "Don't move," she hissed, as dark shapes slunk out of the gloom and surrounded them.

"Holy shit," one of the men said. "Lenars!"

"Stand still," Selena said softly, holding up her right hand.

Shadow looked up, then abandoned his meal and came to stand between them and the other lenars. The creatures circled Selena and the others for a few moments, then regrouped facing Shadow. They nuzzled and rubbed against each other for a moment or two, then turned and melted back into the forest.

"I don't bloody believe that," Braxis growled, as there were sighs of relief from the other troops

The battlenet erupted in Selena's ear. "Captain," Arthur said. "There's a small craft approaching quickly. Friend-or-foe says it's Federal but it's not responding to our hails. It should be with us any moment."

Selena's brow furrowed as she thought it over, then with realisation her eyes widened. "Take cover!" she shouted, as adrenaline surged through her. But before anyone could move two of her men were blasted from their feet by machine gun bullets. Pain exploded in Selena as she was spun around with a bullet in her right shoulder. Flung against a tree she collapsed to the ground, while Braxis fired up into the darkness from a kneeling position. As six figures landed with gravpacks Braxis took several of them out before he was hit and blown backwards. Selena looked to where her machine gun was laying in the grass a few feet away, but knew she'd never make it. The pistol was on her wounded side and the handle of her sword protruded over her right shoulder. She couldn't draw either, and if she did they would stand little chance against assault rifles. A familiar figure strode forwards and smirked down at her, as she tried to stand upright.

"Muller," she said.

"Not so clever now are you?" he grunted, as his men gathered round. He nodded towards her wound. "Hurt, does it? I owe you remember? Oh, yes, I forgot to tell you. My brother and I hadn't fallen out at all, we joined up together but then he got sentenced to the Penal Corps for smuggling. I was hoping to gain your trust, so I could kill you myself. I'm going to enjoy every little bit of your suffering."

Shots rang out and Muller went down, as did another of his men. Braxis had been badly wounded but managed to open fire from where he lay. Selena reached across her body for her pistol with her left hand but before the others could react dark figures sprang out of the trees. Selena watched as lenars dragged the struggling and terrified men off into the darkness. Their screams of terror and agony tore at her ears but were quickly silenced. Braxis hauled himself over the terrain towards his commander. He helped Selena up as they both glared at Muller who sat in the grass, blood stained from two bullets to the chest and a thin ruby trickle coming from a corner of his mouth. Then Shadow appeared out of the darkness and stood nose to nose with him, growling ominously. Muller tried to push himself away, coughing up more blood. He looked at Selena as if unable to understand what had just happened.

"Muller, I warned you..." she sighed, reaching down and stroking Shadow. Her smile, when it came, was feral. "Dinner," she said.

*****

"General, what's going on?" Selena demanded, over the battlenet. "Muller just tried to kill me."

"That doesn't make sense," Magki replied immediately. "Where are you? You're not showing up on our scans, they've gone haywire."

"We're still at the nest."

"Dillon, we've got inbound FOM ships and lots of them. I need you and your men back here, pronto, we're under attack."

Then the net went silent.

Selena turned to Singh and the others. "Looks like the regulars are up to their old tricks and are trying to take

Capulet, now the Manta have gone. Separating us from the general and sending a team after us must have been part of their plan."

"Which means they'd have probably killed us too," Cox gasped, wiping his brow yet again. His brown eyes widened with fright and the beads in his beard jingled as he spoke.

"Death frightens you, does it?" Selena asked him.

"Well, yes actually…"

"We'd better get out of here, Ma'am," Arthur said. "When they don't hear from Muller the FOM may suspect we're still around, and if they saturate the area with troops they're bound to find us sooner or later. We also need to meet up with any others who got away from the city."

Selena raised her eyebrows. "You're actually starting to sound like an officer, Arthur, and you're right. Can we use the skimmers?"

"Aye, Ma'am, if we keep them in stealth mode below the trees and away from prying eyes."

"This is only a flesh wound," Singh said, applying a battle dressing to Selena and binding it tight. "The bullet went straight through. The doctor will patch you up when we get back, but Braxis is going to need some rest. He was lucky. You both were, much more so than those other poor devils."

"He can rest when we're on the skimmers. Now let's get out of here." Selena slipped her arm back into her tunic and did it up, then put her arm into the sling Arthur fashioned for her.

"What about the lenars?" Singh persisted. "You know what happened last time we flew low."

"Oh, I don't think that's going to be a problem," Selena replied, pointing into the darkness between the trees, where long dark shapes stood watching them. "They didn't harm us at all, but they sure took out the regulars. I'm not sure what's going on but I think there's more to them than we know, and Shadow has a hand in it all. Let's get out of here. Head towards Capulet city, our people there need our help."

Aboard the skimmer Braxis lay unconscious on a pallet on the port side, while Selena sat on the starboard equivalent. Shadow lay curled up next to her, head on her lap, and as the skimmers slipped silently through the trees the lenars paced them on either side, a few leaping from tree to tree. They hadn't gotten very far when there was a sudden flash from the direction of the Manta building behind them, and a brilliant ball of flame boiled into the sky. Selena's expression darkened and they carried on in silence. When they were fifty miles from where the alien building had been they stopped and took a break. Selena gathered them round.

"Braxis is still out," she reported. "It's pointless taking him into a fire-fight, so I'm leaving him here with the scientists and four troops for protection. Arthur, stay here and take charge. Singh, myself and the others will go on ahead."

"Captain," Arthur said. "I have Lieutenant Kotes calling us on shifting pattern Charlie. He says he's hiding just outside the city and the regulars have seized the *Magellan*."

"Let me speak to him." She keyed in the frequency for Charlie channel. "Kotes?"

"Captain, it's good to hear from you. As I told Arthur, the regulars launched a surprise attack. They've captured the city and the *Magellan*. Luckily, I was having lunch with a few friends and they smuggled me out."

"What's the state of play regarding our men in the citadel?"

"I'm told the General and our troops are under armed guard in the palace grounds," Kotes replied, "along with the Queen and her militia. Obviously the Federal government didn't like her joining us and ordered the regulars to seize the planet."

"You say she's being held in the palace grounds?"

"That's right Ma'am, in her accommodation."

She turned to face Singh, to find him returning her look with an odd smile on his face. "Funny how things come around," he said.

"What's that supposed to mean?"

"You know exactly what it means. The person you hate most and tried so hard to kill is now on our side, and it looks like we'll have to rescue her again. Now that's just plain ironic."

She ignored him and turned to Arthur. "A change of plan, you're coming with us."

*****

Luckily, the sewers emptied into a river that carried the knee-high effluence out to sea. All they'd had to do was cut through the thick metal bars installed originally to keep marauding lenars out. A short distance from the entrance they passed the sewage treatment plant and from there on it got unpleasant, the stench was unbelievable.

For Selena the journey was a trip down memory lane. Years ago, she and her cohorts entered the sewers from within the city and tried to assassinate the Queen, but now they had to wade through the cloying muck until paths appeared either side of the slow-flowing liquid. She knew while her troops were grateful for the help of the lenars they were also pleased the creatures remained behind near the river. The only lenar that came with them was Shadow, who Singh held above the stinking liquid mess in his arms due to Selena's wound. Finally they arrived at their destination and Selena looked up the ladder at Arthur as he worked busily on the alarm system in the torchlight. Around her, the troops blended into the darkness.

"Torches out," she ordered. With a loud click Arthur finally slid the cover aside, revealing a dark, cloudy night sky. "Remember," she whispered, "knives if possible. We use stealth until we have no other choice."

One by one they climbed the ladder, Selena waiting below until one of the men lowered a rope with a sling which she put Shadow into. The trooper pulled him up quickly, while Selena climbed up the ladder nursing her shoulder. They lay prone under the bushes in the palace gardens, studying their surroundings. The musky scent bought back bittersweet memories. Selena shoved them aside and pointed to a guard patrolling nearby. She whispered into Shadow's ear and he slunk off. Suddenly the guard vanished without a sound, as the lenar took him by the throat and dragged him under a bush, clamping his jaws about the thrashing man until he stilled. Shadow remained where he was, flattened against the ground and invisible.

Selena and the others rose to their feet and, keeping low, ran over to the gym. Arthur dealt with the access panel and then stepped away with a nod, to indicate the all clear. With their chameleon suits blending into the brickwork, Selena raised her hand, silently counting to three by pointing her fingers, and then they stormed in. Troops with beam weapons immediately shot the startled regulars guarding the prisoners. Other captives from the Penal Corps took advantage of the uproar to seize two other guards, taking them prisoner.

"Is that you, Dillon?" a voice called.

"Yes General, it's me. If you could get the men to grab these weapons we've bought with us, along with those from the guards, we've a city to retake. In the meantime, as much as I really dislike the idea, I'm going to make sure the Queen is safe."

Leaving the general to organise his troops Selena and the others padded through the gardens to the Royal Quarters. "Getting to be a habit, this," she remarked under her breath, then she turned to Shadow. "Stay here and guard our exit, in case we need it." In reality she was more concerned he would be killed in the confines of the corridor behind the security door in front of them.

Arthur did his magic with the access panel and on the count of three they took the guards by surprise and quickly killed them. As they raced over the bodies one of her team raised a beam weapon and pointed it at a door that hadn't been there the last time Selena was here. They'd obviously increased security.

"No," Selena hissed, pushing the woman's weapon down. "The doors are reflective, trust me I know."

They put on the breathers they carried, knowing from Selena's brief that during her assassination attempt an unknown gas-type weapon had rendered her entire team unconscious.

Arthur checked the readings on his handheld and shook his head, it was completely clear. There was nothing to indicate a chemical or biological weapon. He opened the dark-brown satchel he carried and took out a small box and held it against the lock. "Nanobots," he whispered, stepping away to stand with the others as they all watched.

The lock dissolved in front of their eyes and again Selena counted to three, holding her fingers up for all to see. On the third count her troops wrenched the doors open and four of them dived onto the thick dark-green carpet beyond, firing their weapons at the regulars who stood frozen with gaping mouths. Two of those around Selena fell in the brief cross fire and she tripped over their bodies and landed badly, wrenching her injured shoulder. The sickening pain as her wound tore open again and blotted her black uniform made her gasp and then grit her teeth. The Queen and her guards were sat bound in chairs, their mouths taped shut. Singh strode forward and savagely ripped the tape away, as Arthur helped Selena up. The Royal Guards mumbled under their breaths while the Queen winced and shot Singh a furious look, before saying to Selena, "Captain Dillon, well, well. It appears I owe you my thanks. Now, if you'd be so kind as to release us?"

For a moment no one else moved. Selena looked at Singh. "Cut them free," she said coarsely, then turned her back and walked away, cursing but knowing she had no choice but to leave her unharmed.

*****

General Magki looked up from his desk as Selena and Shadow entered his office, a smile on his face. "Captain Dillon, welcome. What's more, well done! You did a fantastic job. The city is back in our hands and it's the FOM Regulars' turn to be imprisoned in the gym." His booming laugh echoed. He gestured to a chair and said, "Sit down, we have to talk. The Queen has spoken highly of you."

"Has she, really. Somehow I doubt that."

His cheerful face went sombre. "Look, I know you've had issues in the past..."

"*Issues*? That bitch is directly responsible for the death of my parents. There's no way I can forget or forgive that! Could you? She's lucky I didn't put a bullet in her head while she was tied up. It's only because the Admiral ordered me to ensure she's still alive when I leave this hole that she's even breathing." Besides Selena, Shadow issued a low rumbling growl, marble eyes fixed on the general.

Magki ignored Shadow. "Put your feelings aside, Selena. You may hate her guts but she's bought Capulet onto our side. That's why the Federation tried to invade, they couldn't afford to lose this world. Being on the main trade routes it's in a highly strategic position. Oh, and by the way, the Queen's banned all lenars from the palace grounds, under any circumstances. She says she lost too many of her ancestors to them and the thought of the lenar's give her nightmares."

Just then the screen on the desk in front of the general lit up. He glanced down immediately. "What is it?"

"A flotilla of ships from Loreen has just arrived, Sir," a woman's voice replied, "a light cruiser, four destroyers and twelve frigates. They're moving into orbit now. Wait, damn it. Another group has just appeared furthered out. They're Federation Regular ships, Sir. Seventy five in all, including what looks like eight assault carriers."

The general looked stricken. "Tell our ships to remain in high orbit, together with planetary defences they put us in quite a strong position. Selena, you'd better come with me." The general rose and quickly led the way to a darkened command room, screens covering the walls showed the enemy ships inbound and their own vessels overhead. All around them men and women, including Arthur, manned numerous consoles, each with fraught but determined looks on their faces. "Tell Lieutenant Kotes to get the *Magellan* into orbit and to join the others, we need every ship and weapon we can get."

The woman suddenly shouted: "Sir, they're attacking our computer systems, though I don't know how."

The general turned to Arthur. "Lieutenant Jones, sort it out."

"I'm trying, Sir," Arthur replied. "They got in through a back door and tried to seize control of the AI. I've patched in a backup system, but we're operating at about thirty percent."

"Damn," Magki spat. "That means we've only a few sunbeams and point defence guns to protect the city."

"More ships have arrived in system, Sir. There's one dreadnaught class, four heavy cruisers plus twenty-one others. Looks like they're ours and may have been tailing the enemy, they're attacking the carriers."

"Thank God," Selena breathed a sigh of relief. "It's still not great odds. Forty four of ours, including the

Magellan, against seventy five but at least we have the satellite defences as well."

"Tell the flotilla to remain in orbit," the general growled, before adding more quietly to Selena, "Don't forget our systems have been upgraded and, as far as we know, the Federation fleets haven't. We also have those new deflectors. Shame those damn battle stations I ordered haven't arrived yet."

"Three of the carriers have been taken out, Sir," the woman reported quietly. "Two more are damaged, one critical. Federal units are peeling off and countering."

"Sir, something else has come into the system." A voice from the dark added.

"What do you mean *something*?" the general bellowed. "Explain man."

"It doesn't make sense, Sir. It's as though it keeps changing shape, like a blob the size of a small moon, and there are ships with it. My God, those are Manta."

A panicked buzz of conversation rose in the room, until the general told them to quieten down. All eyes were on the screens, and you could feel the tension as they watched the huge blob break up into dozens of smaller ones. The aliens stopped and held their position, apparently watching the conflict and perhaps waiting to engage the victors. Then out of nowhere five enormous ships appeared, again of unknown origin, and immediately attacked the Penal fleet, their weapons cutting through the vessels and their defences easily. Selena and the others gasped in horror as several of their ships blinked for a moment and then disappeared from the screens.

"I don't believe this," Magki growled. "Those were top-of-the-line ships, with all the latest upgrades. It's a goddamned circus. Who, or rather what, are those?"

"I imagine it's the ForeRunners, who else could it be?" Selena replied. "They're obviously helping the FOM. Wow, take a look at the Manta, they've gone ballistic.

They're attacking the ForeRunners but those allies of theirs are holding off. Sir, tell our ships not to attack the Manta. They've not done us any harm yet and as the saying goes *the enemy of my enemy is my friend*, at least until this battle is over. At the moment we have a common enemy. If we support them perhaps we can swing the Manta to our side."

There was a deathly silence throughout the room, as the General considered it. "You're right, Captain. I'm requesting our ships support them but keeping the flotilla in orbit above us, just in case."

They continued to watch in silence as the Manta continued to attack the ForeRunner Craft, aided by the Penal ships. Then the Federal ships joined in the melee and utter chaos reigned. Realising they were outgunned the Manta and penal forces began to withdraw but were chased. Immediately the Manta's allies took up stations between them and their pursuers. Foolishly the FOM attacked the newcomers, only to have their fleet swatted aside, leaving the unknown ships and the ForeRunners slugging it out in a phenomenal show of power.

One of the ForeRunner craft broke away and sped towards Capulet. Instantly the Manta and penal ships swung about and engaged it. Already damaged the enemy craft fought back, destroying numerous craft, but the sheer weight of the combined fleet was too much for it. Suddenly, it succumbed in a blinding explosion and an hour later it was all over.

Only a few of the Federal ships managed to get away, along with just one of the Forerunners craft. Of the Penal ships that had attacked the FOM fleet only thirteen survived, including the now badly damaged dreadnaught. As the ships moved away from the cloud of debris the Manta and their allies regrouped and headed for Capulet. Magki immediately ordered the orbiting flotilla to move between the aliens and the planet, but to hold their fire. Both fleets stopped, facing each other, while the dreadnaught and her escorts took up stations behind the aliens, effectively sandwiching them.

"Looks to me like we've got a standoff," Selena observed.

"Whoever the Manta's allies are," Arthur said, "we haven't a chance against them. Let's hope they're not here for trouble."

"Are they in planetary weapons range?" Magki asked.

"Just outside it, General," Arthur replied. "If they come in close enough we could easily take out the Manta, but seeing what damage their friends did to the ForeRunners I doubt very much we could hurt them at all."

"Sir," Lieutenant Roberts interrupted, "One of those large globe ships is moving towards us."

"Just one?" the general queried. When the woman confirmed it, he told them to let it through and for everyone to continue holding fire.

Moving slowly through the human ships the orb continued to change shape and colour. It penetrated the planet's atmosphere and slowed still further, finally landing gracefully outside Capulet City.

"I guess now we find out," Selena said, biting her bottom lip.

"Roberts," General Magki addressed the young dark-haired woman. "You're in charge. Dillon, you come with me."

*****

Feeling somewhat vulnerable, Selena stood in front of the globe ship, next to Magki and with an oddly calm Shadow at her side. The lenar obviously wasn't frightened of the strange craft, which puzzled her. Both officers bore only side arms but Selena really wished the general had allowed her to keep her assault rifle.

"Something's happening," she observed.

Although she'd seen the vessels before they still baffled her. They were just plain weird, a liquid form that could change colour and shape apparently at will. As she watched one of the seahorse-like creatures emerged from the ships skin and drifted through the air towards them.

"Not very big is it, about the size of a cat," the general muttered softly.

Selena bit her lip and looked at him. "Something like that, but a darn sight more dangerous." Then she noticed something she hadn't before. What she'd taken for stripes on the newcomers were actually gossamer straps that held tiny devices on them.

A feeling of warmth flowed through Selena and a voice echoed in her mind. "We've come with our allies to talk to you."

Selena held her breath but even as she did so a Manta stepped from the alien ship and strode boldly towards them, the glowing orange sphere appearing over its right shoulder. The Manta stopped next to the other being and remained still, and then a voice issued from the orb.

"We don't understand. You are one race and yet you fight amongst yourselves, and those you battle with side with our ancient enemy. Explain."

"Well, that's easier said than done," Selena replied, earning herself a frown from the general.

The seahorse-like creature's many eyes did a weaving dance amongst themselves, akin to a snake's mating ritual. Then the voice issued from the Manta's sphere again. "We are few now and offer no threat to you. Let there be peace between us. We mistook you for the ancient ones. Yes, you are complicated."

The general seized on the moment immediately. "Yes, we would like to have peace. War is no good for any of us but we need to talk about this in greater depth. In the meantime, it would appear your enemy has become ours. The ForeRunners attacked us while supporting our enemies. Our people are now split into two. Perhaps," he gestured to the seahorse, "your friends could act as mediators. What do we call you?"

"We are Sken," the seahorse creature replied. "There is another issue. Your race is guilty of invading another sentient beings world and causing much suffering."

"We are?" the small Korean officer answered, looking confused.

Shadow climbed to its feet and padded over to the Sken, turning its beady black eyes back on the humans. Suddenly Selena realised what it all meant.

"The lenars?" she gasped. "But they attacked us when we landed and have killed a great many of our people. They have no buildings and no literature. They're not sentient...are they?"

"They are nomadic and need no buildings but yes, they are what you call sentient. Their lives are spent hunting in the forests. When your people invaded they defended their lands, then did the same again more recently against those you call the Manta. We are what you call telepathic. You in turn have language, yet the lenar are empathic. They communicate by emotion and feeling. Your adoption of this one you call Shadow surprised them. It showed you can indeed work together, as we all can.

"Now, we must go. There is much for us all to think about. We will speak again soon." The Manta and Sken turned about and walked back to their craft, slipping through its skin as easily as entering fog. Then the alien ship lifted silently from the ground and was gone.

Chapter Nine

On her way to the hospital with Singh to visit Braxis, Selena thought back on the latest developments. General Magki had informed her that the aligned worlds were meeting on Emerson, a small frozen world orbiting Bernard's Star, one which the Manta had not so long ago tried to conquer. She'd only been there once on a fleeting visit and certainly wasn't fond of red dwarf systems, she found them far too cold, even in the underground cities built to protect the inhabitants against sporadic solar flares. Magki told her the Manta and the Sken had also been invited, and it was hoped they would join what had become the Assembly of Worlds.

"Braxis," Singh said abruptly to the nurse at reception, surprised there wasn't a robosec there instead.

"I'm sorry?" the startled brunet replied.

"We've come to see Corporal Braxis, one of our men. You can't miss him. He's built like a mountain and has a face like a very bad boxer. Here's his official number and DNA."

Singh passed her his handheld. The nurse perused his details before checking her records. "Ward five, along the corridor down there to the left," she informed them blindly, whilst passing back Singh his handheld.

Thanking her, the two made their way into the ward and soon found Braxis. He was sitting up in bed, arms crossed with a grim expression on his face.

"What's up with you?" Selena asked, pulling up a chair. "Someone steal your teddy? We just popped in to see how you're doing."

"The bastards won't let me out until tomorrow," Braxis growled. "Thanks for popping in. Did you bring any grapes?"

"No, I think Singh made them all into wine." Selena replied, keeping a straight face.

Braxis eyed Singh. "Bring any wine, Lieutenant Commander?"

"The Captain's led a sheltered life, Braxis," Singh replied. "I constantly amaze her with my ingenuity at being able to make alcohol from just about anything, but as to your question no, sorry. How are you doing? You seem okay, although you had us all a bit worried for a while."

"I'm hard to kill, Sir."

"Well, those Feds nearly achieved it," Selena said. "You were lucky, with those wounds you could easily have died. When you've finished malingering, report to Singh here back in the arena. I just popped in to see how you were. He'll update you on what's been happening. It's good to see you're all right. Oh, and thanks for what you did back there." She patted his arm and left the two of them to chat. She had a job to do.

Selena climbed aboard the skimmer waiting outside. Shadow climbed to his feet from where he lay in the craft and welcomed her by nuzzling her hand. Cox sat sweating behind their driver and a guard, his eyes glued to the lenar. He appeared fascinated.

"Relax," she said, "he won't eat you."

Cox blinked at her in surprise. "Is that an attempt at humour? The lenars don't enjoy the best of reputations, you know."

"Are you going to be all right with this?" she asked, leaning forward until her face was inches from his. "If not, I can soon find a replacement."

The scientist snorted. "Like hell you can, we both know you'd struggle to find anyone else to come along on this little jaunt. People are too frightened of these creatures."

"And you?"

Cox met her gaze. "To be honest I'm scared beyond belief. But then I've you to look after me haven't I. If you can't, who can?"

The skimmer rose and shot over the city walls, heading out into the surrounding forest. Selena waited until a sudden warm glow enveloped her, and then she knew she was in the right place. *Here,* something felt in her mind.

At her command the skimmer stopped and landed in the thick, rough grass. The driver and guard remained in the vehicle as Selena, Cox and Shadow walked a short distance into the woods and then stopped to wait patiently. Dark shapes flitted through the trees and moments later five lenars stood facing them, while Selena knew others remained hidden in the shadows.

"I've come to offer you a truce," Selena began, "a chance to prove we can live together in peace. The general, our military leader here, has spoken to our Queen and they would like to confirm we will not cause your kind any further harm. In return we'd like your promise to do likewise. Both of our races have suffered for too long at each other's hands. While we were once new to this world, this is now our home too, and we're hoping our races can co-exist peacefully.

"Naturally we'll require resources, such as wood, water, minerals and so forth, but we're more than prepared to set aside conservation areas for you which won't be infringed. Galactic Law will protect them and it will be enforced. If there is anything else you need, you only have to let us know and we'll be happy to help."

She felt their understanding and then their agreement, a warm feeling of joy suffusing her. Turning to Shadow, she said, "You better go on home now, back to your people. You're better off with your kind than you are with me." Dropping to her knees she stroked his silky fur and looked deeply into his marble eyes. "I'm gonna miss you, fella."

She felt tears gathering and blinked them away quickly, realising suddenly how much Shadow had come to mean to her. It had been a long time since she'd had anyone to care for, apart from Bryn, and their time together had been far too brief. Shadow filled a void in her life and she didn't want to face the loneliness again.

As she knelt in front of him Shadow planted both forepaws on her shoulders and licked her face. She knew then he wouldn't leave her. He needed to be by her side, as proof that both races could get along together. She ruffled his short fur then looked over to Cox, as he recorded everything. To her surprise he put his handheld away and walked up to the five lenars. They remained still, watching as he stood in front of them. Then he too sank to his knees and held out his arms. One by one the dark, forest creatures came forward and rubbed themselves against him before turning back and melting into the gloom amidst the trees. Aware of how afraid he'd been of them Selena felt nothing but growing admiration for him, knowing what a brave act it had been.

"You're sweating," she said, straight faced, as they stood and walked back to the skimmer.

"Very funny," he replied, wiping his forehead with an already damp cloth. "You're lucky. It could have been a lot worse."

*****

Back in the city Selena stood in General Magki's office, both watching the sunset and the coming of the night through his wall-length window.

"The people here are delighted at the development with regards to the lenars. They've always been terrified of them, so this agreement is quite a turn up for the books. Who'd have thought they were a sentient race?" He turned to face Selena. "I'm still surprised you took Sweaty. If anything I'd have thought you'd have preferred to have Arthur with you."

"I get the feeling Arthur doesn't like the lenars, Sir," she said.

"Why not?"

"No idea, but then he never has been particularly fond of animals."

"Well," Magki replied, "each to their own. You can't blame him, the lenars killed a lot of people but then we did the same to them. I see Shadow's still with you, should help considerably." He met the lenar's dark beady eyes for a moment before looking away. "Anything else?" he asked, suddenly.

"Nothing much, Sir. I think my work here's completed and I was wondering when I can return to Loreen? There's a lot to do back there."

"Your work here's done when I say it is, Captain. We've achieved a lot in this short space of time and I want you to remain around a bit longer. The Manta and Sken ships have left the system now. Off to Emerson I should imagine. The meeting's due to take place tomorrow. It's quite a historic occasion. A peace settlement between the worlds of mankind and alien races, who'd have thought it?"

His screen burst into life, Lieutenant Roberts blurting, "Sir, another enemy flotilla is approaching the system. There are three assault carriers and ten escorts."

"Damn, don't they ever give up? How many ships do we have in orbit?"

"Five," Roberts replied. "The others have returned to Loreen for repairs, or gone to Emerson."

Magki cursed before turning to Selena. "You'd better follow me, Captain."

Back in the command centre Selena watched the enemy vessels approach on the displays. Suddenly one of the Penal flotilla in low orbit exploded. "Damn it! Where did that shot come from?"

"Sir, the satellite defences have opened fire on our own ships," Roberts gasped.

"What?" the general gasped. "Shut them down."

"I can't, it's the secondary system Sir. Something else is controlling them."

"Then take them out, now!"

"Aye, Sir."

"Arthur," Selena said into the battlenet, "problems. Get to the command room immediately." Her order was met with silence. *Damn*, she thought, *where was he?*

Sunbeams from the city illuminated the satellites. Their deflectors held for a few moments, before failing under the combined attack from the orbiting craft and planetary defences; but by that time another ship had been lost. The enemy escorts engaged the three remaining vessels in orbit who fought back valiantly, aided by batteries from the city. Selena felt a moment's surprise that the enemy hadn't come in on the other side of the planet, then realised they wanted to capture the city and to do so had to take it quickly, before reinforcements arrived in system. She watched as the enemy ship losses began to mount, but it was too late, the assault ships had already launched their landing craft and thousands of Federal troops were on their way down.

"Captain Dillon," Magki said. "See to the city's defence."

"Yes Sir. Shadow, stay here and look after the general, you won't be any good up there on the walls. You," she addressed one of the soldiers manning the defence controls, "turn on the dazzlers."

Brilliant beams, as bright as daylight, were directed away from the citadel itself to illuminate anything coming near, and blinding anyone looking directly towards it. Selena wiped her mouth with a bare fist. This was going to be tough. She ordered her men to the walls, ensuring battle droids reinforced them every hundred feet or so. At least a little earlier she'd had the foresight to set up fall-back points throughout the city, just in case. Arthur should be here, preparing a few surprises for the enemy, as he had back on Loreen when rebels had attacked them. Without him she was running out of options.

"Here they come, Ma'am," Braxis said from besides her, pointing up at growing points of light in the night sky. "Point defence should be able to take them out, and the auto guns any survivors who manage to bail out."

She faced him and frowned. "Braxis, you're supposed to be in the hospital."

"I'd prefer to be on the walls, Captain. It's no good waiting in bed for some twat to come and splatter you. I'd rather fight here alongside my friends, if you don't mind."

"Okay, just don't die on me," Selena replied with a splenetic snap, but deep down she was both relieved and touched by his integrity. "Oh, and it's good to have you back. Now get to the walls and out of my goddamned way. Gunnery, take out those landing craft."

Above them the swarms of small craft were met with sustained point defence fire and the night sky filled with beams of light and tracer. Ships fell by the dozen, until those following moved further away. At a safer distance they opened their bays and dropped their troops into the depths of the forest, the enemy soldiers slowing their descent with their gravpacks before landing amidst the trees and running towards the city. Others preferred to skim above the treetops using their gravpacks. Even as the surviving landing craft shot back towards the heavens they were torn from the sky by the heavy fire from Capulet City, exploding or falling in flames into the woodland, where they shattered the trees and ripped them from the ground. Brilliant blossoms of fire rose from the forest up into the sky as they crashed and countless Federal troops were thrown aside by the blasts, yet those who remained in one piece climbed back to their feet and stormed from the forest towards the city walls.

Suddenly the point defence and auto-guns fell silent.

"General," Selena gasped into the battlenet, "can you tell me what the hell's going on? The defences have stopped firing."

"Something's over-ridden their commands. They're down. It's up to you to stop the assault, Selena."

She swore and ordered her men to open fire. Shells and beam weapons slammed into the enemy ranks. Yet still they came on. Thousands of troops shot over the treetops on antigravs, while even more poured from the forest floor.

"Give them everything you've got!" Selena yelled, assault rifle hammering in her arms. "Grenades!" She ordered. The resonating 'crumps' echoed through the citadel, as those with grenade under-barrels fired streams of explosive projectiles from their weapons secondary armament. Others launched their friend-or-foe hand-held explosives which, once activated, shot towards the approaching enemy. The battlements around her rang with explosion after explosion and ricocheting rounds. Besides her a female trooper burst, covering her in bloody and smoking gore, as a microwave beam hit her. Selena ducked down and waited a moment, then jumped up and opened fire yet again at the enemy. Suddenly a red light appeared on her weapon and began to blink before her gun clicked emptily and the light remained a constant vermillion.

"Christ," she gasped. "I'm out of ammo, that doesn't happen often." Dropping behind the walls she ejected the spent magazine and fitted another. The weapon cocked itself and the light turned a solid green. "Four hundred rounds," she muttered. "Would you believe it?" As she was about to stand a dozen or so enemy soldiers with gravpacks shot overhead, firing downwards as they went. Around her several troops fell. She returned fire, watching with deep satisfaction as the small explosive rounds tore into their bodies or exploded in the packs on their backs. Those who were hit yet remained alive dropped the hundred or so feet, screaming all the way to their deaths.

Several of them actually made it to nearby buildings, where they took cover behind whatever they could.

"Damn," Selena growled, gazing down her barrel. Fingering a button on her weapon a sniper scope snapped into position in front of her eye. Peering through it she saw one man poke his head out from behind a metal shed. She fired, watching as his head explode like a rip melon. Someone on the walls besides her had the bright idea to fire grenades at the survivors and chunks of the buildings rained down into the streets below, taking the enemy soldiers with them. Extra commandos' joined her on the walls and added their firepower to the slaughter and gradually the enemy ranks began to waver.

Even Selena was stunned when hundreds of lenars erupted from the forest and swept towards the attackers. Within moments many of the troops were down and the lenars were tearing them to shreds. They all could hear the soldiers' agonised screams from atop the walls. The attack faltered and those of the enemy still using gravpacks turned back to help their fellows, but in many cases were unable to fire into the mishmash of bodies for fear of hitting their comrades. Selena smiled with grim satisfaction, the fools should have kept coming. Stopping just made them much easier targets. Within a short time not one enemy remained, either standing or airborne.

"Cease fire," Selena said into the sudden eerie silence, watching for a moment or two as wounded enemy soldiers tried to crawl to safety away from the heaving throng of lenars. "We're done here. Everyone, get out there and police those bodies."

Braxis looked from her to the prowling lenars that still tore into their wounded enemy. "You're kidding, right?"

"Nope but that's everyone except for you, Braxis. Get your lardy arse back to the hospital. I'll see you in the morning."

"Ma'am," interrupted a female voice she'd come to recognise. "The lenars are leaving. They're going back to the forest."

"You're Lieutenant Roberts, from the command centre?"

"Yes Ma'am. I got kind of bored back there and felt the need to kill some of these bastards."

"Well, Lieutenant, perhaps you can explain to me how the FOM managed to land troops here, given our weapon capacity? How our satellites turned against us and then to top it all the damn city defences went down?"

"That's easy," she replied, watching Selena coolly, "sabotage. The enemy must have a spy here somewhere, somebody with authority who knows our systems."

*****

General Magki joined Selena and Singh as they walked through the dead and dying on the ground in front of the city. Every now and then a shot rang out. Spotting Arthur she huffed a white cloud on the now chill night air and walked over to him, as he searched the enemy bodies as if looking for something.

"Arthur, I've been searching for you...What are you doing?" she asked.

"Just keeping my eyes open for intel, Captain. Anything to let us know why the defences went down."

"Huh, any idea how many dead there are?"

He stood and looked around; hands on hips, then shook his head. "I've no idea yet, but an awful lot by the look of it."

Selena noticed how steady his hands were.

Lieutenant Roberts saluted and spoke to Magki. "General, what's left of the enemy ships are leaving the system."

"Thank you," Magki replied. "With luck this will make them think twice before they try again.

"We have a lot to thank the lenars for," Selena said. "I think you'll agree they've proved their loyalty, General."

"They certainly have," Magki agreed. "As far as I'm concerned they can have their reserves and anything else they need." He paused for a moment before adding, "I'd like to suggest setting up colonies for them on other worlds. Do you think they'll go for it?"

"I think they just want to be able to roam this land in peace, they're probably not interested in anywhere else. But in the meantime…hey, Arthur, have you any idea why the satellites attacked our ships?"

"I'm a genius, not a clairvoyant," he grunted, "but if I was to hazard a guess I'd say they hacked the backups we were running. If I'm right it means they would have identified our ships as hostile and caused the satellites to opened fire on them."

Selena washed her face with dry hands, and rubbed at her tired eyes. "Okay, makes sense but do you have any idea who could have done that?"

"You're joking, right? It could have been anyone, most probably done remotely from one of the enemy ships," he replied.

"Not possible," Roberts interrupted. "The firewalls would have prevented that and would have alerted us to any such attempt. It had to be someone who was there and who could overcome the safeguards."

Selena pulled her side arm and pointed it at Arthur. "Well, if I was to hazard a guess I'd say that was you. What I can't figure out is why."

Suddenly Shadow took to her side. He rumbled and stretched his neck towards the Arthur, who turned a deathly white and stepped back as the lenar bared its teeth. Roberts relieved him of his weapons.

He looked shocked. "What…don't be ridiculous, why would I do a thing like that?"

"Now there's a good question, all along my instincts have been screaming at me not to trust you. I've thought about when we were talking to the Manta, after the battle with the lenars. Like I've said before, we were doing okay until they saw you. It was when the Sken came to rescue them and the first time we saw their weird protoplasmic ships. The Manta were carrying chrysalides towards one of them, remember? Their whole demeanour changed when you appeared. I understand why now, and should have paid more attention to Shadow here and why you didn't like having him around. All rather stupid of me, really. You're one of the ForeRunners, aren't you?"

Her team looked from one to the other, then drew their weapons and pointed them at Arthur.

"You're talking rubbish," he replied with a half laugh, stepping back even further while eying the circling and watchful Shadow. "You damn well know who I am. I was with you during the attack on Mantis." He spoke calmly, licking suddenly dry lips, his concern about the lenar obvious.

"It would explain everything," Selena continued. "Do you want to know what I think? That our Arthur really did die in the battle of Mantis. I believe whoever, or whatever, you once were climbed into that robotic shell and waited for Henry to arrive. When he did you downloaded the data he carried and then destroyed him. You cloned Arthur and waited in that plasteel casing until your body had completely reformed, only then discarding your outer shell. Our trust allowed you to sabotage the satellites and our other defences."

"You're wrong," Arthur snapped.

"Oh, I don't think so. But you didn't take Shadow into account, did you?" Selena continued. "He's empathic, remember? I just couldn't figure out why he really disliked you. I guess he knew exactly what you are and, as I got more used to working with him, I've finally realised what he was trying to say."

"My DNA will check out, test it."

"We already have and you're right, it does, but that doesn't mean a thing now does it? We knew a long time ago the Manta hit your race with a weapon that prevented you from reproducing. It meant you had to work on extending your lives whilst trying to find a cure, hence the reinforced bone structure to help prevent injuries. Manipulating DNA must be nothing to you. It's game over as far as I'm concerned. So, what do we call you?"

He was silent for a while, his eyes lingering on the lenar. Finally he said, "Arthur will do, why not? Yes, we knew your lieutenant was dead and also that he was a genius. It was a good gamble you'd accept our story, and you did."

"For a while," General Magki replied. "You're under arrest for endangerment, spying and being a member of a hostile government. Lieutenant Roberts, take ten men and escort our guest to the cells. Ensure he remains in full view and under armed guard at all times. As for you, Arthur, we'll speak later."

"Unbelievable," Singh muttered, as Arthur was marched off. "A real live ForeRunner and our Arthur really is gone. He never did feel quite right, but I just put it down to him being killed, something like that would screw anyone up."

Together they walked through the dead and dying, watching as shots rang out and the bodies were piled into skimmers and taken away to a site a few miles away to be burned to fine ash with beam weapons. To Selena's sorrow she saw many lenars laid there too and ordered the troops to collect them and lay them side-by-side in the foliage of the forests they loved, and where their bodies truly belonged. In the distance, oily acrid smoke began to rise from the funeral pyres.

Singh stopped for a moment. "We complain about the Federation showing no mercy and yet look at us. Perhaps if we showed them some they'd reciprocate. The stench of blood, death and burning bodies, it follows us around."

"They'd still kill us," Selena replied. "These are shock troops and the enemies finest. They don't take prisoners, end of story. If we let them live and eventually released them we'll only find ourselves fighting the same people a short time later, and they'll be killing what few friends we have left. Do you want that on your conscience?"

"Not at all," Singh replied. "It's just, well, wrong."

"Yes, I know. But think about the people we lost at Bernard's Star, when they took us by surprise by planting those bombs on our ships and then mopping up what was left. They didn't warn us or ask us to surrender. We have no choice. It's either kill or be killed now."

Selena saw Shadow staring right back at her, and felt his horror and despair at the loss of his kin. There were few of them left now, so many killed in recent weeks. Yet she was aware they knew they had to stand their ground and fight for what was theirs, or risk losing it altogether.

As one they turned back to Capulet City, watching the flags and banners flapping noisily atop the fortress walls. Even from where they stood sentries could be seen patrolling them. A strange despair filled Selena. This had once been her home. It was where she'd been raised. Her father had been murdered here and she'd seen her mother commit suicide, leaving her all alone in the world except for her Aunt May. She knew who was responsible and they would pay. Just not quite yet, she could wait.

Until then another home beckoned, one called Loreen. Even that thought brought sorrow, for Bryn had asked her to settle there with him, on the side of a beautiful crystal-clear lake in a home which Franks had agreed to build for them. But that was before Bryn died, and the dream was long gone now.

What worried her most was that if Arthur was really a ForeRunner what did it mean for Hope, who had the same skeletal anomalies? Was she a ForeRunner too? If so, who was going to tell give her parents their daughter was probably dead and there was an enemy doppelganger in her place?

Chapter Ten

Arthur looked up from one of the three lime-green comfortable looking armchairs in his cell. "Hello General, come to gloat? Ah, Selena you're as gorgeous as ever," He said, legs crossed and peering over the top of his steepled fingers, and elbows on the arm rests. "What news? Please..." He gestured to the other chairs.

As they sat General Magki replied, "As you ask, an accord had been reached on Emerson between all parties concerned, including the aliens. We've forged an interstellar organisation called the AOW, or Assembly of Worlds. Mutual defence had been agreed in principle but we've still some way to go yet. It looks to me like you could be on the losing side."

"I doubt it," Arthur replied coolly.

"Oh, you think so? We've told them everything we know about Eden and the rabbit holes. We did this to ensure they understand Eden's importance, and so help us protect Loreen. Let's face it they'll be helping us to explore those worlds when all this is over. Having them aboard is a great idea, especially since those planets once belonged to you. "

"They still do."

"As we see it," Selena joined in, "Loreen is going to become a major hub for our colonisation projects and, unlike you, we intend to share everything. We've been completely honest and open with everyone, and that includes the Manta and Sken."

Arthur was silent for a moment, still watching them over his fingertips. "And what did they say?"

"Why, they agreed of course, why wouldn't they? The AOW have unanimously approved funding for whatever Loreen needs, in addition to pledging ships and troops. Oh, and the Sken informed the Assembly that in ancient times your race, the ForeRunners, rampaged through the galaxy murdering many of the races that had been around at the time, including the inhabitants of what we now called Arcadia. We're told the Sken also had access to that world but were too far away, exploring places we can't yet imagine. The one or two ships they had in the area arrived far too late to help the inhabitants. It was they who dug up those burial mounds our people found, and which the caretakers had been so busily trying to hide when they learned visitors were on the way.

"So you see your secret out and I'm sure the Federation will find out soon too, so much for your little secrets. The Sken are back here in force and they tell us that out of all the ancient races only the Manta stood up to you, but when they did the cost to both sides was horrendous. Billions of lives were lost and many worlds destroyed. It was then the Manta released a plague that scythed through your race, until only a few were left. Arthur, we know you eventually found a cure for that illness, but the disease and the treatment itself sterilised what few survivors there were."

"Yes," Arthur snapped. "That's exactly the point isn't it, we survived. But it's an existence of the worse sort. We can't have children nor can we clone ourselves, despite all of our knowledge. For some reason when we try it reactivates the plague and both the foetuses and hosts die. You're also right there aren't many of us left, so when just one of us is killed it's a major blow to the whole race. Rest assured though, there are enough of us still around to do what we need, and we have what you call the caretakers."

"Let's face it, you got your asses kicked," the general interrupted. "So much so you fled rather than be eradicated, and when you'd gone the Manta had to go into hibernation." Magki paused dramatically. "When they finally awoke it was to find mankind trespassing on what was once their worlds and, mistaking us for you, they struck without warning. Is that about right?"

"Almost, but you don't understand," Arthur snarled, his face contorting. "The Manta are a virus! They were spreading so quickly and taking new worlds we desperately needed. You have a very blinkered view, General. You need to appreciate we were defending ourselves and you need to do the same. For what it's worth, I don't understand why the Manta hasn't used the virus against you, it would certainly work. Perhaps they had a guilt trip after what they did to us or, more likely, the Sken stopped them. Remember, it only needs a few Manta to survive and they'll breed millions in no time at all. You humans almost destroyed them once and if you don't exterminate them now they'll spread throughout the galaxy. Trust me in this, in time they *will* come after you and when they do there'll be no way you can stop them."

"What about the Arcadians and the other races you wiped out? Protecting yourself against those as well, where you?" Selena asked, sweetly.

Arthur ignored her.

"Tell us about the Federation of Man," the general said, to fill the sudden silence. "I'd really like to know why you're helping them."

"It's quite simple really," Arthur replied, putting one leg over another and bouncing the foot up and down. He no longer wore the black uniform of the penal corps but bright-yellow prison coveralls and, bizarrely, matching slip-on shoes. "We want Loreen back. The technology we left there was experimental. What you call rabbit holes lead to every world in our empire.

"During the plague we lost so many people we had to abandon Loreen. The Manta were surging through our territory and we had to pull back quickly. You can't even begin to imagine what it was like to watch billions of your people dying all around you and wondering if you'd be next. Whole cities and planets were laid waste. There were ships floating in space filled with our dead and dying, and we had to destroy those vessels rather than let them fall into enemy hands. Luckily we managed to disguise the entrance to the rabbit holes when we left, and when we found your people had discovered it we had no option but to take action. We allied ourselves with the Federation of Man on the understanding that Loreen is returned to us."

"The FOM don't know the truth about Loreen, do they?" Selena asked.

Arthur drummed his fingers together, watching them both carefully. "Okay, so we may not have been completely honest with them, but that's politics for you. We offered to help them and that's all they were interested in. Let's face it, all the Federation wants is humanity restored, under their control of course."

Selena spoke up. "If that's the case what made the Federation attack us in the first place? Why didn't they just talk to us? We fought besides them, we're their own people and yet they attacked us when we least expected it. Yes, we're one race and originally there was no bad feeling between us. So why did they do it? We lost a lot of people and surely, if anyone, you'd know what that feels like."

Arthur leant back in his chair and burst out laughing. "Just think about it, you're just a bunch of criminals trained as fighting machines, much like the gladiators of your Ancient Rome. Yes, of course we've studied your history. You're ravening beasts, twisted by war. The FOM knew that one day you'd be turned loose on society and they were afraid, and who can blame them? So all it needed was a little push from us to decide your fate. Let's face it, we all know what to do when there are dangerous animals around. You cull them, pure and simple. They were simply protecting themselves. And just so you know, we *will* have Loreen back," he leant forward, glaring intently, "no matter what you think. It's only a matter of time."

"I'm afraid you're sadly disillusioned," Magki replied. "There's no way you'll get Loreen, nor Capulet. Vast numbers of reinforcements have begun arriving and we've started building the battle stations to help defend this world. When the Federation and your people come back here, and I'm sure they will, they're going to get one hell of a shock. On a different tack, I have a little theory you might be interested in."

Arthur sat back and raised a smug eyebrow. "Something that might interest me? Oh, I sincerely doubt it."

The general ignored him and continued. "Let's for arguments sake say we believe you, that the Manta sterilised your entire race, and your advanced medical knowledge enabled you to eventually make yourselves relatively immortal. After all, you can even replace your skeletal structure, so God knows what else you can do. But even so, your numbers are still falling. Let's face it accidents happen and then there's battle attrition, and so forth. Then lo and behold, far from being alone out here, you find a race of descendants you didn't know about before. Now I'm not into gambling but I'd bet a fortune you hope you can breed with humanity and reverse the damage the Manta inflicted on you.

"Then there's the fact you suddenly have millions of people to fight your war, in return for certain technology of course. That's quite an incentive to side with the Federation against us, and certainly for them to side with you. Any thoughts?"

Arthur's face was inscrutable, as he replied, "I'd say you have a vivid imagination, General. If what you say is true what do you think the Manta would do if they found about such a medical possibility? They'd destroy every human world they could, including your so-called Assembly of Worlds. They won't trust any human no matter what they say, and so your fragile peace won't hold.

Surely even you can see that? Your people are stuck between the proverbial rock and a hard place, with us on one side and the Manta and their friends on the other."

"So if you were in our shoes what would you do?" Magki asked, at length.

Arthur made a show of inspecting his fingernails. "Why I'd make peace with the ForeRunners and the Federation, of course. Like you said, we're all the same people. It's just that we're far more advanced than you humans are. We should all work together and rid the universe of the Manta, and of course it goes without saying our demands about Loreen stand. Even with our ships, which are so much more advanced than yours, it takes a long time to reach many of our worlds by such conventional methods. As much as I hate to admit it the Sken ships are faster than ours. Loreen has our instantaneous transportation technology and that gives us an advantage. When we have it back we'll be able to rally our forces and defend any of our outposts more easily."

"Surely," Selena interrupted, "if we were allies then you wouldn't mind us staying on Loreen, now would you? Particularly if, as you say, we're all part of the same race. Perhaps there's a way we can work out a settlement and even make peace with the Manta and the Sken."

"What part of this don't you understand?" Arthur snapped, his eyes blazing furiously. "Loreen is not negotiable! You either leave that planet immediately or we'll sterilise the whole world with weapons you can't even begin to imagine. Believe me when I say their use will haunt you to the end of your days, and then we'll take Loreen anyway."

Selena raised her right middle finger. "Do you know what this means? No? Well let me enlighten you, it means 'fuck you and your whole goddamn race'."

*****

"The battle stations are up and running but it'll take a couple more months before they're completely operational," General Magki said to the senior officers seated around the dark, wooden conference table. Along the light-tangerine wall were pictures of spacecraft, with their names in little tabs at the bottom. "In the meantime we now have a battle group of over a hundred ships from all over the AOW in this system. You've all heard what the ForeRunners have said about Loreen. We've warned them and the other worlds to expect an attack, and we've beefed up defences everywhere as much as we can. We stand a good chance against the Federation ships on their own; it's the ForeRunners that really worry me. In the meantime, the Queen has something to say."

Standing up the Queen looked at each of them in turn, before saying in a clear piping voice, "I've approved the building of five new bases here on Capulet, one at each of the North and South Poles, and the remainder equidistant around the equator in line with our city. They'll be fitted with major weapons to provide backup to the orbital platforms when they're operational, and as these bases are completed others will follow.

"Until now we've deliberately kept our population to a minimum, rather than risk the starvation which affected so many other worlds, when population explosions caused havoc. Now we need people to man these new installations and to build our cities. Consequently, I've enhanced benefits to families with multiple offspring, in the hope this will lead to a growth in population, which in time will fill those new facilities and the cities around them. I've also released more land for farming. It's hoped we can recruit workers from other worlds within our new Assembly and they'll bring their families with them. I've no doubt many will remain here when the cities are completed. They'll certainly be plenty of employment for them. We need to build and protect our planet, and I'm asking for your help in this. Capulet is a strategic world, and I'm offering it to the Assembly of Worlds as a major military base."

Selena pushed her chair back and stood, looking calmly at the monarch as she sat back down at the end of the table. "What of the citizens, Majesty? Where do they stand in all of this? Our people's lives are going to change dramatically and not all of them are going to like it."

"They'll appreciate being alive, and they are not *our people* they're mine!" the Queen snapped. "This is about the survival of Capulet and I think when it's put in context they'll realise this is the right thing to do. Whatever you think of me, bear this in mind, I only want the citizens of this world, and humanity as a whole, to survive this war. If that's wrong then history will judge me, not you."

Chapter Eleven

Selena strode back to her tent in the arena. She'd been offered one of the rooms available in the new accommodation blocks springing up nearby, with the city's walls being pushed out even further. The tent smelt damp and it could get cold at night, so she'd quickly accepted and would be glad to move. At this rate of expansion she knew the city would soon be infringing on the forest and was worried what that meant to their relationship with the lenars. Shadow stirred in the darkness at the end of her bed as she undressed and she felt suddenly suffused by warmth, which meant they understood the importance of what was happening to the city. It would be okay. Naked she reached down and gently stroked Shadow's short, tufty fur.

"Thank you," she murmured and planted a kiss on the top of his velvety head. Just then a light flicked into life on the small screen on the table she used as a desk. A quick look told her it was Kes, so she keyed the accept button.

"Wow, Selena. You sure know how to answer a call."

"I thought you'd have seen enough of my breasts, Staff Sergeant. What do you want?"

"It's Lieutenant now and, hey, no disrespect Ma'am but I have to say your chest is magnificent. I just rang to see how you were. Heard you had some trouble and I was worried about you and the others."

Selena burst out laughing. "You, worried? Ha, ha, give me a break. You just wanted a perve."

Kes grinned from ear to ear. "I certainly did." He grew more sombre. "I miss you, Selena. I know how much you loved Bryn, but...well, never mind. It's just kinda hard not being around you."

Selena fell silent for a moment. "Let's get something straight Kes, a shag is a shag, you could have been anybody. Just because I fucked you doesn't mean I'm falling for you. As far as I'm concerned you and I are just friends, it'll never be any different and I thought you'd have realised that. Looks like I made a mistake, sorry but that's the way it is."

Kes looked hurt for a moment but then covered it up. "I know commitment's hard for you Selena but you need to understand all of us love you, some more than others." He paused and looked more closely at her. "Hang on, I know you...something's up. Tell me what's wrong."

"It's Arthur. Believe it or not he's a bloody ForeRunner. Our Arthur really did die. This one just has his memories."

He sucked in his breath. "Damn, I hadn't heard but I guess it's been kept under wraps. Look, I've got to go. You take care and remember I'm thinking of you...and the others."

"Don't go all soft on me, Kes. You'll only get hurt and you know it, and neither of us wants that. Before you disappear, how's the course going?"

"I've finished it, flying colours by all accounts. They're sending me to Loreen next. Anyhow, give my regards to the guys and let's chat again soon."

"Aye, congrats anyway, Lieutenant. I knew you'd make it. Take care." Selena's felt her eyes sparkling with pride as she cut the connection.

Braxis burst into the tent. "Captain," he blurted, ignoring her nakedness. "Arthur's escaped!"

"What...how did that happen?" She quickly climbed back into her uniform and followed him out of the tent flap.

"Nobody knows. I'm afraid the guards are missing, presumed dead. Shit..."

The both automatically ducked as around them the defence batteries burst into action, firing brilliant beams into the heavens. Amidst the stars the barely operational battle-stations opened up too. Selena and Braxis ran to the control room, where Singh confronted them.

"It's the Federation and ForeRunners. A large combined fleet arrived in the system a few moments ago. They took one look at what we had waiting for them and fired salvos of planet busters at us. Luckily, the defence stations managed to take the missiles out. If those stations hadn't been in place we'd all be dead now, or facing another invasion."

"What of the enemy, where are they now?"

"They've gone, Captain. They fired and left the system. Something odd happened though, a small transport lifted from the space port just before they arrived and rendezvoused with the enemy. Whoever it was left with them."

"Arthur," Selena said, her lips thinning. "It has to be."

"You're kidding me, right?" Singh gasped. "We had him all locked up safe and secure. It doesn't make sense, how could he get away?"

"That, Lieutenant Commander, is a damn good question. His guards are gone too. They're either dead or they were in on it. Arthur's out there somewhere, and he's no longer one of the good guys."

"You know what this means, don't you?" Singh asked, his face torn by anxiety.

"Oh yes," Selena replied sadly. "I've already ordered Hope's arrest and that of her parents, or at least until we can prove their humanity. After all, they were alone in Arcadia too."

*****

Explosions rocked the city, causing blossoms of light to flare through the side of the tent. Selena threw herself out of her bunk, rolled and grabbed her weapons. Luckily, she'd remained dressed and so was out of the tent within moments. She stopped short as Braxis ran towards her.

"What's happening?" she demanded.

"General Magki's dead, Captain. Several of the defence platforms have been disabled and the Queen is demanding to speak to you. Looks like sabotage."

"I've better things to do than speak to that old hag."

"With respect Ma'am no, you haven't. We need to keep her sweet and you're now the senior officer on this whole blasted planet. You've no choice, you have to see her."

"Damn!" Selena was piqued by the truth of the matter. Together they ran to the Command Room, where everyone stood to attention as she entered.

Selena bit down on her frustration. "Lieutenant Roberts, put me through to the Queen." As the screen lit up to show the monarch, Selena said, "You wanted me?"

"Thank God you're alive, Captain," the Queen replied. "I thought for a moment they'd gotten you too. You're the senior officer now. I want you to take command."

"Pardon me but I understand Admiral Anderson is in orbit, he's the most senior officer present and if anyone needs to take command it should be him."

"Anderson's good but he's a fleet man and he's in charge of our assets up there. You know this planet, the people and a whole lot more. You will take command Captain, that's an order."

The Queen had her over a barrel and Selena knew it. She hadn't specialised for either the army or navy yet, and wouldn't need to until her next promotion. Then after further training she'd become either a Commodore or Brigadier, if she lived long enough.

Selena leant forward and glared into the screen, well aware of the people behind her. "With respect, Ma'am, let's get something straight. You have no rank in our military, so I don't have to take orders from you. Of course I'll comply with the orders of Admiral's Anderson, and Van Pluy. They are my direct commander's. If they order this then so be it. I'm not trying to be difficult, Your Majesty, but there's a chain of command to follow."

The Queen relaxed. "Thank you for being candid, as always, and I understand. However, I'm not concerned with our past problems. It's the safety of the people and this whole planet that's important. I'll await Van Pluy's decision, although I can guarantee he'll agree with my suggestion. Good day, Captain." Then the screen went dark.

Selena felt the palpable silence behind her and turned around to face her crew. "Haven't you lot got anything to do? If not I can soon find you something. Braxis?"

"Yes, Captain?"

"Arrange for my belongings to be moved into the new accommodation blocks. Speak to the Quarter Master. He'll let you know which room I've been allocated. Then tell him I want the rest of our team billeted near me. If he has any problem, send him to me."

"Captain, you have a call from Admiral Van Pluy. You may wish to take it in your...in the General's office," Roberts said.

"On my way." In a few moments Selena was sat in the general's chair, watching as the screen lit up. "Admiral, what can I do for you?"

"I think you already know the answer to that. The Queen called me and has requested you take command of Capulet, says you're unhappy about it. Personally I can't see that, but you're in charge now. Do I make myself clear?"

"You certainly do Sir, although I can think of several others far more suitable."

"Well, I can't, Selena, and to be honest I don't give a toss what you think. You're it, end of story. The Queen made salient points, and I happen to completely agree with her. We can't afford to lose Capulet. If we do it'll send a bad message to the Assembly, so you need to do whatever it takes. By the way, the enemy fleet that visited you did a fly by here too, no doubt scoping us out. They were in and out as quickly as possible, so I guess they realised they've no chance of capturing Loreen."

"Well that has to be good, particularly after what Arthur said. Don't worry, Admiral. I won't let you or the people here down."

"I know you won't," he replied, a half smile on his craggy face. "There's one more thing before I go. As you *suggested* I've had Hope arrested. She's under armed guard in the citadel itself and her parents are staying with her voluntarily. They both checked out, we already knew they didn't have that skeletal structure. As you can imagine they're not happy."

"I imagine you've explained about Arthur, Sir. The ForeRunners have the ability to recreate their bodies in another's image, including all of their memories."

"Yes, I told them and thankfully they understood. The main issue is how to tell if Hope really *is* their daughter. We just don't know enough about the enemy cloning process."

Selena said her goodbyes and turned off the screen. She cursed lightly, unsure what she could do about Hope. As for taking military command of Capulet...well, there was nothing else in the pipeline and they were correct, she was the right person for the job. She just hoped she could avoid killing the Queen in the meantime.

*****

The first thing Selena did in the morning, after having settled into what had been the general's office and accommodation, was to speak to Admiral Anderson and request the workers building the battle-stations be put onto double shifts. Thankfully he agreed and work went ahead at a much faster rate. Already the deflectors and most of the weapons were operational, it was just the cosmetics that were taking the time.

Selena was delighted to see the Queen's attempts to recruit workers from the AOW were already paying dividends. Hundreds arrived daily and she found huge satisfaction in the rate the new construction sites were progressing. The thing that concerned her most was saboteurs. They'd already struck once when they'd disabled the defence platforms and assassinated the general. Despite all efforts they were no closer to identifying the culprits. Then an idea struck her.

"Shadow? Do you think your people could help us?"

By now the lenar had grown to her mid-thigh. When it looked up at her she knew he understood and would ask his kin. He got up and left the room on his way to the forest. An hour later he was back and sat looking up at her, with all six paws on the floor. She could feel their agreement, on the understanding the lenars were only loyal to the penal regiments. It was them they trusted. She immediately spoke into the battle-net. "Lieutenant Roberts, my office."

The small slim, dark haired officer soon stood in front of her.

"At ease, Lieutenant, take a seat. I have a task for you."

Robert's looked surprised as she selected a chair. "Anything I can do, Ma'am, just let me know."

"Just so you are aware, Roberts, I did some research on you. I was curious as to why the general kept you so close."

Her dark eyes chilled. "And?"

"You were a professional assassin, employed by criminal gangs. I was actually quite surprised by that. Never caught, the only evidence against you came from someone who squealed to save themselves. Strangely he's dead now, I checked."

"It was a miscarriage of justice, Captain. They never proved anything but sentenced me anyway."

Selena ignored her and carried on. "It says here you're responsible for at least seventy kills. Quite a record you have. Now the reason I've said all this is I might need to call on you one day, although it won't be anything too dramatic. How would you feel about that?"

Roberts watched her closely. "It all depends on what you might want."

"We'll discuss it when the time comes. Anyhow, all this has nothing to do with why I called you here today." She eyed the multitude of tattoos from the top of Robert's right shoulder down to her elbow, and then ignored them. "I understand you have an affinity with animals, not that Commander Muller would have appreciated it. Given your gift I want you to create a small group of twenty people or so, to work with the lenars. We're going to use their empathic powers to root out these saboteurs. The ball is entirely in your court, Lieutenant, but I suggest you start by selecting between fifty and a hundred people from our ranks. Not all of them will be suitable."

She glanced at Shadow, before returning to Roberts. "There will be twenty lenars waiting outside the city walls in a couple of hours. Handpick your team as soon as possible and start work. I'm not interested in how you do it, only in success. If you need any help then say so. In the meantime there are other things I need to be concentrating on. Shadow here will go with you to put people at their ease, but bear in mind that each lenar will only bond with one person."

Roberts looked somewhat daunted but then her face relaxed and she reached down to stroke Shadow. "He's really quite cute."

Selena hid a smile. "Somehow I'm not sure he'll find that a compliment."

*****

Within two days Roberts made her selection, which included herself. The training really was getting the lenars and humans used to working together, accepting their partners as an equal and learning to read each other. She set each team tasks, starting with patrolling the city.

Late on the second day there was a knock on Selena's office door, interrupting her assessment of how well the work fared at the new defence establishments. "Come in," she said, turning away from the screen. "Ah, Roberts, some good news I hope? Take a seat." The lieutenant did as she was bid and Selena noticed she was almost bouncing up and down.

"Yes, Ma'am, I've very good news actually. Your idea's working, we've already caught two saboteurs."

Selena breathed a sigh of relief. "Excellent. Tell me about it."

"Both are civilians but one is Federation through and through. He's ex-military who settled here some time back. He's the one who killed the general, says it was his duty and he was just following orders. The other is a young lady who was being blackmailed. They have her family imprisoned on Mars. She says he had no choice and either she did what they said or her family would suffer. She's already admitted sabotaging the platforms."

"There's always a choice. Okay, I want an immediate high-profile military trial. It's to be televised and both are to be found guilty. The girl will be sentenced to five years imprisonment. The man is to be executed immediately the trial is over and his family are to be sent the bill for the bullet. If his family have any assets here I want them confiscated."

"Very well, I'll see to it." Roberts watched Selena closely.

~ 156 ~

"Examples need to be set, Lieutenant, but this girl was trying to protect her family, which we can all understand. Now, as your search teams are working so well together I want two teams assigned to each city or base. Send the others up to the battle-stations and ships in orbit. I want all of them searched. After all, we can't be too careful. I'll clear it with the admiral. Once they've completed those tasks I want them back down here."

Just then the wall screen burst into life. "What is it?" Selena snapped, angry at the second interruption.

"Captain," a harassed private began, "Loreen's under attack."

Selena sat bolt upright in her chair. "Are you sure? That world's far too well defended. They wouldn't dare risk those defence platforms, I'm sure they're aware of their firepower."

"That's precisely it Ma'am, there are thousands of crab-like robots coming out of the tunnels. They've already overrun the base camp on Eden. Most of our people managed to escape but it was only the auto-guns and troops we placed in the tunnel here that stopped them breaking out of the rabbit hole. The admiral's rushing reinforcements there right now."

"Keep me informed of all developments," Selena snapped. Turning off the screen she thought: *Damn it, I should have foreseen that. By coming up through those damn tunnels they bypassed our planetary defences. God, how stupid can I get?* She dismissed Roberts with a wave of her hand and immediately called Admiral Van Pluy.

"Selena, you've heard?"

"Just now Sir, I'm sorry. I should have seen it coming. It's obvious when you think about it. No wonder Arthur was so confident they'd get Loreen back."

"Well, don't blame yourself. We should all have seen the possibilities, especially me, although I don't think the enemy realise how many people we have here. All being well we should be able to contain them in the tunnel. It's if they get out we'll have a problem. I've told our people to set up fall-back positions and overlapping defences all around the entrance, and to mine it in case everything goes pear-shaped. It's interesting the ForeRunners are using the caretakers rather than risk themselves. Thankfully they seem quite limited and are just trying to break out. The fact that there are no Federation troops with them suggests they've still not been informed about this rabbit hole technology, or they can't get them to the other end of the tunnels. Either way's quite lucky for us."

Selena thought for a moment. "The caretakers previously recognised us as ForeRunner descendants and followed our orders. They must have overwritten those settings to make the machines see us as enemies, which also suggests they'll see any Federation force as enemies too. Perhaps that's why there's no humans at all amongst them."

"Excellent point," Van Plus replied, "and worth considering. By the way, Lieutenant Phillips is in the thick of it. He's a good man."

"Thanks for letting me know, Sir. Tell him to keep his head down. I have to go now, but I look forward to catching up soon."

*****

Selena had the new bases on Capulet built quickly by focusing on three main areas: the perimeter walls and power rings to protect the workers from any attack, basic shelter and a landing pad, then weaponry and power supplies. In the short term the workers' families remained in Capulet City, at least until the basics were completed. Food and water was flown to the stations daily. All in all it worked very well.

It was early evening when Selena received a call from a major, speaking on behalf of Admiral Van Pluy. He introduced himself as his new personal assistant. "Forgive the intrusion, Captain, but the Admiral asked me to call and update you on the situation here."

"All's well, I hope," she replied.

"Not really. The caretakers are still coming through the tunnels in their thousands. They have some kind of beam weapon that incinerates our men. A simple touch and they burst into flame. You could be standing next to someone then suddenly find him burning to death besides you. It's horrendous what they're going through out there." The man shuddered for a moment before continuing. "They're like a constant wave, clinging to the walls and even the ceiling. The firepower pouring into the rabbit hole is horrendous. Your Lieutenant Phillips has thirty men constantly firing streams of grenades down it. All they're doing is firing, reloading and firing again. Even with those explosions and the heavy weapons we've got in place, plus the troops' personal weapons, we're only just keeping them at bay. Kes asked the admiral if we could bring a sun beam weapon down from one of the ships and use it to fire at them."

"Yea gods," Selena gasped, shocked at the thought. "What did the admiral say?"

"He said 'no way, the facility was far too valuable and the weapon might destroy it by accident'. He also pointed out that if we win this battle but began to lose the war we can always retreat down those tunnels to safety and blow them up behind us. We've orders to hold on all costs. Captain, at this rate we'll be running out of ammunition in a day or two, although we're expecting supplies from the colonies."

She slammed her fist on the desk, feeling helpless and frustration lacing her voice. "Is there anything I can do?"

The major shook his head. "No, you just look out for Capulet. Hang on…" He put her on hold and then came back on the line looking relieved. "I've just heard the flow of the enemy is slowing down but we don't know why. The admiral's ordered us to prepare a frontal assault, in the hope of creating a bridgehead in Eden. They're going to be preceded by a swarm of bees to ensure we're not running into an ambush. Intelligence is concerned that the presence of the bees might tip off the enemy of our intent, so once they've shown all's well our troops will pour down the rabbit holes. Now I'm sorry, Ma'am, but I have to go. There's so much to do."

"Yes of course Major, and thank you."

"You're welcome," he replied with a curt nod. "Take care."

She sat watching the darkened screen for some time. It was no good, she went and found Singh in the dining hall. Sitting beside him she ordered a coffee from the steward and updated Singh on what was happening.

He looked stunned. "They must have lost thousands of those machines by now. Kes will be okay. He's one tough cookie, and by the sound of it he's doing a terrific job. The sunbeam's a great idea, although the admiral has a point."

"He sure does," Selena agreed. The smell from the chilli he was eating made her feel hungry and suddenly she realised she hadn't eaten since the night before. Placing an order with the steward for the same dish and a glass of chilled white wine, Selena said, "Have you heard what the Queen's calling the new cities?"

"No," he replied. "But judging from your tone I gather it's going to be interesting."

"She has a thing about Shakespeare, keeping in vogue with the rest of this place I guess. The city at the North Pole is now called Roussillon, the southern one is Ephesus and the one directly opposite us on the other side of the planet is Elsinore. To the west is Navarre and to the east we have Messina."

Singh snorted, a spoonful of chilli and cheesy potato halfway to his mouth. "Are we supposed to remember all that? I suppose it was too easy to name them A, B, C and so forth. Or even North, South, East and West."

Selena burst out laughing. "You don't change, do you?" She grew more serious. "I wonder how thing are going on Loreen."

She found out six hours later. No longer able to stay awake she forwarded her calls to her room, left her office and retired for the night, sleeping on top of the bedding fully clothed. When the screen pinged she wiped the sleep from her eyes and swung her legs from the bed, before sitting at the desk and accepting the call.

"I thought I'd call to update you, as there have been quite a few developments here," Van Pluy greeted her.

"Thanks, we've all been concerned. I was just getting some rest."

"It looks like you need it, no offence intended. In the meantime there's good and bad news."

"I hate it when people say that," Selena replied, combing her hair with her fingers.

"As my PA informed you, the enemy numbers coming through the tunnels has been reducing but a short while ago they stopped. We sent a swarm of bees ahead of the assault group. They showed us there's utter carnage in Eden."

"In what way?"

"The Sken were there in force, attacking the caretakers. Those weird ships of theirs were strafing those robots and our base camp has been utterly destroyed. Many of the trees are...well, shattered. The things those Sken ships fire are unlike anything we've ever encountered. Those projectiles don't explode, they eat everything they hit. That includes trees, foliage, the enemy — everything. There's a lot of scattered metal and bare earth.

"We saw the ships stop their assault and thousands of Sken came out of the forest and engaged the caretakers. It was an incredible battle. Those beam weapons the caretakers carry are horrendous. Our people went through and joined the fight. Apparently a group of ForeRunners tried to flee in a dozen or so small craft, but the Sken ships bought them down. Here's the feed from the bees."

Selena watched the screen, as it showed a few survivors climbed from the wreckage of the ForeRunner ships, only to be incinerated by the caretakers. "Looks like they couldn't tell the difference between our DNAs after all," she said. The battle lasted a little while longer, but before long it was all over and the filming stopped.

"What happened then?" Selena asked.

"Several of the Sken approached our people and told us they'd found the rabbit holes on Arcadia and followed them back to Eden. Seeing the caretakers invading Loreen through the tunnels they stuck to their word about mutual defence and attacked. For the first time our forces fought side by side. The bad news, of course, is the Manta will be aware of the battle and will now know the tunnels can be used to bypass our planetary defences. If they decide to turn against us again it could prove our undoing, if they could find a way to get to one of the worlds with rabbit holes."

"Well," Selena replied, "on the flip side maybe it's a good thing. This indicates we can actually work together for the common good."

The admiral nodded. "Yes, well, let's hope so. Either way there's nothing to be done about it now. We just have to be on our guard. I've had the troops begin construction of major defences on Eden and here at our end of the rabbit hole. I guess that's about all we can do. We've been resupplied too, thank heavens. Hopefully we can take a well-earned rest."

"How's Lieutenant Phillips? The men are bound to ask."

The admiral gave her a warm smile. "He's okay and a damn fine officer. I've put him in charge of Eden's base camp. It's a relief to know it's in such capable hands. Now, if you don't mind Captain, I need to get some rest. No doubt we'll chat in the morning, when I'll expect a full update on the situation on Capulet."

"Good night, Sir," Selena replied, releasing a sigh of relief. Not only had she been concerned about her friends, but losing control of Loreen itself didn't bear thinking about.

Chapter Twelve

Selena fretted. She wasn't a diplomat or a desk jockey; she was a field officer and wanted to be in the forefront of the action. Sitting behind a desk kicking her heels was frustrating, but she knew the admiralty was correct. She was the right person for the job and had to accept it.

She'd expanded the search teams to forty and things on that front were going well. Selena had thought about the admiral's suggestion about creating colonies of lenars on other worlds and asked Shadow to discuss it with his people, but as far as she knew they were still thinking it over. Going through her mail she saw the other worlds in the Assembly were already requesting search teams and knew it would be hard trying to deny them, no matter how much she explained the lenars would only serve the Penal Regiments. Both groups now understood and trusted each other implicitly.

Selena pondered the problem for a while. If she could overcome this issue several possibilities occurred to her. If the lenars could be incorporated into police forces they would change law enforcement dramatically, and there were unlimited commercial possibilities. Companies would pay tremendous sums to know what their competition was doing or even whether people attending meetings were telling the truth, and then of course there were politics. Yes, things would change a lot, if the lenars were interested.

Shadow slunk into the office. He'd been down to the forest again. She could feel the waves of emotion, as he stared up at her with those dark almond eyes. She jumped as she understood what he wanted, then got up and left her office, taking Shadow with her.

It was a dull cloudy day outside, as she and Shadow walked through the streets. It had rained only an hour or so earlier and she loved the damp smell of the city. She paused to watch children leaping in and out of the puddles to see how far they could splash the water, or more likely who they could drench.

To Selena's surprise people stopped to watch them pass, mostly with smiles, whispers and even pointed fingers. One or two turned and fled immediately, and Selena knew it would be a long time before prejudice and fear left all of her people. Too many had lost relatives to the lenars. It was only when a young girl reached out and stroked Shadow that Selena realised things were already changing. Fear of the Forerunners and FOM meant that for the first time people were starting to accept the lenars, and from the warm glow emanating from her companion she knew he felt it too.

Reaching their destination Selena keyed the buzzer on the door and a small screen to one side flicked into life. Cox looked at her in surprise.

"Captain Dillon? Come on in."

The door unlocked with a click and she pushed it open. They entered a long and narrow vanilla scented red-walled hall, in which a wide variety of paintings hung. The hall emptied into a luxurious deep-green carpeted apartment, where Cox waddled toward them wiping his brow with a cloth. He was genuinely pleased to see them, she knew this instantly from Shadow. Cox offered her his hand and then stroked her companion.

"While I'm delighted to see you again, Captain, I doubt this is a courtesy call. So, what can I do for you?"

"I need to ask you a favour," she replied. "I just learnt from Shadow that the lenars suffer from some kind of disease, which has been keeping their number down. They know and trust you, so I'd like you to help them. You're well qualified to deal with this, and to be honest I can't think of a better person for the job. You'll have complete freedom in running the show. So, are you interested?"

"Oh, most definitely," he said with a grin, gesturing to several expensive looking sofas. "Please, take a seat. Can I get you something to drink?"

"Jasmine tea would be nice, if you have it."

Only gone for a few moments Cox soon returned with a steaming mug of the aromatic beverage, which he offered to Selena, and a bowl of water for Shadow. She took a sip. It still surprised her how much she'd missed the locally-grown, fragrant brew.

"You're empathic too, aren't you?" she asked, watching as he nodded in agreement. "I thought you might be, it makes a lot of sense. I find it strange we didn't pick up on the lenars' ability when our people first arrived on Capulet."

"That'll be the fear," the scientist replied. "Humans put up barriers when confronted by something terrifying, and of course the lenars attacked because they were protecting their world. Now things have changed and we've discovered common ground, survival. I hope you don't mind me calling you Selena, but tell me what you know about this disease."

"Not much I'm afraid," she replied, "only what I've picked up from Shadow. It's hard to describe how he gives me the information. It's like a feeling, an experience of what's happening, as if you've been there yourself and seen it happening. What I do know is the lenars get sick without warning, and have to be isolated by their community before they can pass it on to others. If they don't act quickly then more catch it and all those who do eventually die. They've lost entire communities. The lenars have no concept of medicine and so didn't understand what was happening to them. I'm sorry to ask this of you, Cox, but as a qualified xeno-biologist I need you on this, and you appear to have an affinity with them."

"You're sorry?" he gasped, looking surprised. "Are you kidding me? This is what I've trained my whole life for. It would be any scientist's dream to be able to work on a project like this. So don't you apologise or worry about it, just give me the resources to do the work."

"Let me know what you want. If I can get it for you I will."

*****

As the days passed and Shadow grew to waist height, the situation on Capulet improved with remarkable speed. The new establishments were up and running in what must have been record time. When their weapons trials passed without issue, Selena ordered the construction of more accommodation blocks and stores, then improved sanitation and power plus the many other things a city needed. Before long their walls began to edge further out, as they grew in size. She soon allowed the workers families to join them and most quickly found employment in the young cities. Selena added more weapon platforms and multiple other projects as the influx of workers swelled even further. But, while delighted with the progress, Selena began to get a nagging feeling she was missing something.

Suddenly it struck her. What would she do if the caretakers struck at Capulet? There'd be no way to contain them once they arrived, but they had to get here first. As she considered the problem Selena decided to have every incoming ship quarantined in high orbit, and checked out prior to landing, just to be on the safe side. But that niggling feeling remained to haunt her. It was desperately important and she knew it.

Frustrated, Selena stood and walked over to the light-grey, top-of-the-range coffee machine in her office. Magki had loved his little luxuries. She typed in an order for a large mocha, while continuing to ponder. Her staff had thoughtfully left a small bag of marshmallows besides the coffee machine and she tore it open and dropped several of the pink and white fingertip-sized sweets into her mug.

She froze, something... Mesmerised Selena dropped even more in and stared aghast as it hit her.

"That's it!" she gasped, stepping backwards away from the machine, shocked she'd missed something so simple. Within moments she had Admiral Anderson on the screen.

"Sir, I need you to launch fighters immediately. We need to have Combat Space Patrols up all the time. We also need the space based defence platforms fitted with multiple long-range small arms."

"You want to tell me what's up, Dillon, or should I just follow the orders of a junior officer?"

She swallowed. "I'm sorry, Sir, my sincerest apologies. It's just occurred to me the weapons we have available in orbit are all anti-ship. We have nothing really to take out much smaller objects, and we need to be prepared for all eventualities."

Anderson visibly bit back his frustration. "For heaven's sake woman, spit it out."

"The caretakers Sir, we're open to infiltration by them from space. Sure our land bases have point defence, but if the caretakers get into the system somehow and come down in the forests then we've had it. We need a way to intercept them, hence the long-range small arms on the defence platforms."

The admiral stared at her. "My God, Dillon, you're right." He turned away from the screen and yelled commands she couldn't make out. Then he was back facing her once again. "It's done, Dillon. Fighter wings are launching even now. I'll order the battle-stations to be upgraded immediately. Let's hope it's not needed but it's better to be safe than sorry. That was a good call, Captain."

It was less than three weeks later twelve ForeRunner cruisers appeared in system and shot past Capulet, firing multiple salvos of projectiles towards the planet. Luckily the admiral had a trick up his sleeve, having witnessed these fly-pasts before he'd anticipated such a move and sewn anti-ship mines in the system. He immediately ordered them activated and watched as they locked onto the vessels as they drew close. Within moments five of the cruisers were brief balls of flame in the darkness. Then the battle-stations opened up and their combined heavy weapons destroyed another ship and damaged others. Having fired their weapons the battered survivors slipped back into hyperspace. Fearing the projectiles were planet busters they were quickly taken out, but not until they'd mirved into clouds of much smaller objects.

"Caretakers inbound!" Lieutenant Robert yelled from the control room over the battlenet, a young lenar at her side.

"How many?" Selena asked, calmly.

"All of them, I think. I'm showing thousands," Roberts replied. "They've got something on their backs, probably some kind of anti-gravity device to allow them to land safely."

Selena swore under her breath, but luckily all the space defence platforms had been upgraded and the fighter wings on patrol engaged the machines immediately. Many of the fighters blinked out of existence but then the planet based defences kicked in too. When Anderson called her an hour later it was to inform Selena that not one of the caretakers survived to make it down to the planet.

*****

"Captain Dillon," Lieutenant Roberts said over the screen. "Can you come into the command room please?"

"What is it?" she asked, wishing for just one day where one thing after another didn't demand her attention.

"Just something I think you should see."

Selena pushed back her chair and forced herself to her feet. She was exhausted and knew it, and above all was not in the mood to be played with. She secured the couple of buttons undone on her collar and, leaving her office, strode crisply down the corridor and into the control room, where she stopped dead in her tracks.

Admiral's Van Pluy and Anderson were both there waiting for her, as was the Queen. The room was filled to the brim with troops, who raised a cheer as she entered. Singh and Braxis's eyes twinkled and Roberts was grinning insanely. To Selena's utter astonishment she saw Kes was there too, with Roberts watching him closely.

"What…" Selena managed to gasp.

"Well that's a first," the Queen observed, as the noise died down. "I've never known you to be stuck for words before, Captain."

Van Pluy gave the Queen a warning look and gestured for Selena to come closer. Then he said loudly, "Captain Dillon, on behalf of the Regiments and the Assembly of Worlds, I've come here to congratulate you on the superb job you've done here on Capulet. No one could have done any better. You've proven my point that this world was left in very safe hands. The Queen and I have discussed your efforts in great depth and would now like to reward you for all your hard work."

Selena didn't know what to say.

"He's not joking, Captain," the Queen said, appraising her coolly. "Admiral?"

"You've already received our highest award but today we're delighted to add a bar to your Sunburst, which makes you the only person ever to have received it. Congratulations." Van Pluy stepped forward and gave her a small blue box that was open and displaying the bar to her medal, then he shook her hand.

For a moment there was silence in the room, and then the cheers erupted once again. She realised then how much of a father figure Van Pluy had become. Damn it! She swallowed her feelings knowing any sign of emotion would ruin her reputation, and she knew the Queen was watching. She saluted the Admiral and tried to still her bubbling emotions.

There was a little party afterwards, nothing too extravagant but it was a chance for them all to let their hair down. Selena enjoyed a single flute of champagne from local vineyards, and then went back to her office, followed by the two admirals. She made them both a hot drink and then sat down at her desk, stirring a spoonful of harlequin sugar from General Magki's personal supply into her coffee. Then she said, "Okay, forgive me for being pessimistic but I take it you've come here for a reason other than the award. While I'm sure you know how much I really appreciate the gesture, it could easily have been done by screen. So, if you don't mind me asking, what's up?"

Van Pluy turned to Admiral Anderson. "See, I told you."

Anderson smiled and then said to Selena, "It was an ideal opportunity to come and discuss a rather urgent matter. My comrade here informed me you'd suspect there was more to our visit, and he was right. The long and the short of it, Captain, is that both the Sken and the Manta are demanding the right of entry to the rabbit holes at Loreen, which means access to the ForeRunner worlds. The question is what do we do about it? You have an ability to think outside the box and we'd appreciate your thoughts."

"Let's face it," Selena replied, "the Sken already have access to them from Arcadia, so the answer's obvious. As I see it we should agree to their request. The ForeRunners have kept this technology hidden from the Federation, and our new allies will be watching to see what we do. We can't show ourselves to have the same morals as our enemies. If we deny them the right of access we'll show ourselves as untrustworthy and they could decide to take it for themselves. While we can defend ourselves against the Manta we stand little chance against the Sken.

"My suggestion, Admirals, is to grant them access but again ask they help us to defend Loreen and the rabbit holes in general. I appreciate this is a bit awkward, given our recent war with the Manta and the losses we all suffered, but to be honest I don't feel we have much of a choice."

Selena stood in front of the window, hands locked behind her back, overlooking the city and the forest beyond it as the two senior officers behind her spent a few moments savouring their coffee.

"Those are my thoughts exactly," Van Pluy replied. "Admiral?"

Anderson was silent for a moment but then agreed. "You're both right, it has to be done. If we don't then we risk a war on another front against two very advanced races and, to be blunt, it's a war we couldn't win. While we've given the Manta a battering they're still a potent foe. By agreeing to these requests at least we keep them on our side. All we can do is hope that we're doing the right thing."

"I was going to suggest we put certain safeguards in place," Selena advised. "Such as planting even more thermal bombs in the tunnels and looking to see how we can improve our defences on both sides, on the pretext that should the ForeRunners try again we can destroy the rabbit holes if need be. I've a feeling our new allies won't fall for it but I'm sure they'll understand our concerns and will agree anyway. My Aunt May used to say the only thing to do is suck it and see. I'd also like to see alternate lines of communications open, in case they can jam the ones we have. Maybe we can install land lines and use the bees to carry messages."

"Makes sense," Van Pluy replied. "I'll see to it."

Anderson sipped his coffee. "Putting another few ships into orbit wouldn't stop the Sken, and to be frank we'd be hard pushed to spare those vessels. Every member

~ 172 ~

of the Assembly of Worlds are demanding protection, and while we have them building their own space defence systems and ships we'd be hard pushed to justify taking ships away from them to defend ourselves against our own allies.

"What I've done is create several immediate reaction groups, each protecting a given sector. As soon as something kicks off they'll head straight to the hot spots. If I need to bolster anything it's these, not tie up ships where they won't do any good anyway."

"Okay, then we're agreed," Van Pluy said, "which leaves one final thing."

Here it comes, Selena thought.

"Captain, your search teams have done brilliantly. I'd like some sent to Loreen. See to it."

Selena put down her drink and faced him squarely. "It doesn't work like that, Admiral. The lenars work with us here by choice. They've already declined the opportunity to have colonies on other worlds, although I've suggested this again and they're considering it. Their prime motive for helping us on Capulet is to ensure their survival here. That's all they're interested in."

"Captain, this is not a request it's an order. Make it happen, and soon. Is that understood?"

"Perfectly, Sir: but please be aware I can only ask them, not order them. If they agree, I have the ideal person for the job."

"Who's that?"

"Lieutenant Roberts, she'll dovetail with Kes perfectly."

Chapter Thirteen

Selena, Cox, Roberts and Shadow left the city and trekked deep into the forest. It was strange, Selena thought, for a great many years her people had thought the lenars extinct and yet they'd been here all this time. The group stopped as one, sensing the lenars coming. The long, slim creatures slipped from between the trees like ghosts and stood there facing them, waiting.

"I know you don't understand my words," Selena began, "but you do the feelings behind them. I've been asked if you'll consider some of your people going to Loreen, we're worried about infiltrators. I know you were against this before but we'd like you to reconsider."

"As I'm sure you're aware, the ForeRunners tried to invade Capulet using their caretaker robots but luckily they failed. Because of this they may try to destroy this world. We have a lot of defences set up but it only takes one planet buster to get through and start a chain reaction, then this world will be gone and your people with it."

They felt her feelings and concern and knew it was the truth. In turn she felt their fear, their query about where they could go and what they could do.

"There's not a lot of land on Loreen but there's still enough for you. Those of you who work with us will earn money which can be used to buy property on other worlds where there are forests, so eventually you'll have several colonies. If you like we can look for a world of your own, it's up to you. All we'll need is a few of you aboard the search ships to make the selection."

We are not many now.

She felt the words slip through her mind. Had she somehow linked the emotions to words, or had it developed into a form of telepathy?

"Cox here is starting a project to investigate the sickness affecting your people, to see what we can do. I'd like you to let him know as much as you can about it and take him to any sufferers you have. He'll also need to take samples from you, and see the graves of your people who fell to this disease."

She felt their agreement. "What can you tell me about it?"

We were aligned with who you called the ForeRunners, once.

Selena gasped. "What?"

It was a long time ago, when there was peace in the universe. When war broke out some of them came here and we allowed them to stay. The first time we fought was when the Manta tried to invade this world, and then the sickness came.

Selena turned to the others. "Did you get that?"

Cox turned to her. "The Manta? They used genetic warfare against the ForeRunners, so what was to stop them from using it against the lenars for helping their enemy? This seems weaker than what they used against the ForeRunners themselves, but it's still effective. It also explains why the lenars attacked the Manta in the forest. They must have known who was responsible for their plague."

"Then the Forerunners left them to die instead of helping them, which would hack anyone off. Hang on a moment," Selena replied. "The Manta are supposed to be our allies now. Do you think they might help us to cure the lenars?"

"Wherever we find a cure, it'll give us an extra edge," Cox replied.

"How's that?"

"Because we may well find there's a template. If we can cure one of these diseases we might be do the same with another, which would give us a huge bargaining chip with the ForeRunners; but God knows what the Manta and Sken would think of us."

"It wasn't the Manta that did this, it was the ForeRunners," Roberts said. "I'm not sure how I know this but I do. After the Manta attack was beaten back in that ancient war the ForeRunners decided they wanted this world for themselves. They tried to destroy the lenars using a similar weapon to what the Manta had used against them, but as their own casualties mounted they had to leave anyway. The lenars attacked the Manta in the forest when we were there because they were trying to invade again, and they were protecting their world."

"Good grief," Selena replied. "What a mess. But now the Manta know the lenars are helping us against the ForeRunners maybe they'll help us cure them. Mr Cox, get to work and keep me updated. Lieutenant Roberts, I'd like six teams sent to Loreen and you're to accompany them. See to it."

Roberts eyed her shrewdly. "Very well, Ma'am. Mr Cox, good luck with your research. I hope it goes well, because from what I can tell these thousand or so are the last of the lenars."

*****

Van Pluy looked at Selena from the screen. "What news, Captain?"

"I've done as you requested, Admiral. Lieutenant Roberts is on her way to Loreen with six search teams."

"Good, thank you Selena. How is everything else going on Capulet?"

She bit back her frustration. "Fine, no problems at all, in fact it's going brilliantly. I'll be honest with you, it's a bloody milk run and I'm getting bored. I'm not a desk jockey and you know it. I've got itchy feet."

Van Pluy hid a grin. "Well, as it happens your relief's already enroute and he should be with you in a couple of days."

Selena felt relief wash over her. "Thank you, Sir. Where am I being posted?"

"To Loreen, I have a mission for you Captain." He looked at the expectant expression on her face. "The Sken and the Manta are going after the ForeRunners. Their troopships will be here shortly and we're going with them. I want you to lead our own contingent and to take some of your search teams along. As soon as everyone's ready they'll be going down the rabbit holes. The Sken say they know where the ForeRunners are holed up. This is a seek-and-destroy mission, something right up your alley. Bring your team with you. I'm hoping to get this show off the ground within the week."

"What about men, Sir? I know we're short."

Van Pluy laughed. "The members of the Assembly of Worlds emptied their gaols and sent all of them to us. We rejected a lot of course but a surprising amount got through basic training. A lot of people hate the Federation for what they did during the Manta war, abandoning them and their families to face the bugs alone. Revenge is a strong motive and these recruits have bags of it."

"I suppose the fact that the planets they came from will be saving considerable sums of money has nothing to do with it."

"Captain, you're becoming a cynic. Now get yourself over here as quickly as you can. I have two thousand troops waiting for you."

*****

Roberts and Kes met Selena at Loreen's spaceport when she landed, and their skimmer took them straight to the hill that housed the rabbit hole. Van Pluy was waiting when they arrived and Selena couldn't believe the change in the terrain around the establishment. Everywhere she looked there were weapon emplacements and troops from each race.

"Captain," Van Pluy began. "You're here at last. I've had to hold back the Sken and the Manta, they're raring to go. I've had their forces mass on this side of the tunnel. We don't know what surveillance the ForeRunners may have in Eden and I'd hate to tip them off by massing the troops on that side. Our allies may be more advanced than us but on this world we're in charge. Once you're through those tunnels the Sken will take over and you'll follow their commands."

"Very well. How many of our allies are there?" she inquired.

"Lots of Sken but not so many Manta. It appears they're still licking their wounds from your little party a few years ago. As for the Sken, well it's hard to tell exact numbers. They flit in and out of those amoebic craft of theirs so damn fast it's hard to judge, but there must be thousands of them to say the least."

The admiral looked at Selena and her team. "Be careful. Bring my troops back safely or at least as many of them as you can."

As the admiral walked away Selena was surprised to see a Manta lumbering up to them, followed by a Sken, its eyestalks writhing as it floated in mid-air.

"We go now, yes?" the Sken enquired.

"In a short while, I need to speak to my troops first." She eyed the Manta. Big and black with a livid white scar down the right side of its face, there was something about it. *Ska would be a good name for that beastie*, she thought. To her surprise both aliens waited where they were and, after she'd met and briefed her officers, she told them she was ready and they could move out.

Following the countless Sken soldiers and a multitude of their bizarre amoebic ships Selena led a long line of skimmers up and into the mountain. She was shocked when they arrived at the tunnels. Despite an obvious effort by the humans to clean up, debris from the battle was still around. There were scattered pieces of metal everywhere, along with evidence of explosions and horrible burn marks that made Selena shudder. Even the chamber inside the mountain was blackened, while the guards' desks and chairs had vanished and the old auto guns were simply marks on the walls. Guards stood by the shattered gates watching the streams of allied troops marching and floating into the tunnel. As her skimmer passed they came smartly to attention and saluted.

Selena watched the Sken ships split into smaller blobs and then elongate into long tubes of constantly changing colour that slid easily down the rabbit hole leading to Eden. Next came the Manta, maybe a thousand or so, marching after the Sken and finally the long lines of skimmers with their human cargo followed. Selena had to admit the sight was impressive. Then her craft joined the line and entered the tunnel, and she checked her weapons yet again.

Moments later they were out of the tunnel and into the sunlight of Eden, where even more Sken waited to join them. The troops manning the defences at the far end came to attention and saluted her as the skimmer flew past. The tented base camp was flattened and the entire site looked like a still from a war movie.

"I wonder why so many of the Sken and Manta are walking," Singh muttered. "The Sken certainly have enough craft to give everyone a lift."

"Maybe those ships are full," she replied. "Or it could be a status thing, or some kind of ritual."

"Singh, you can't blame them about the Manta. Would you want something that ugly on your ship?" Kes asked.

"Well, we've got Braxis with us," Singh jibed. "Hopefully the bad guys will take one look at him and surrender."

"Hard de har, har," Braxis growled. "You should be grateful I'm on your side."

They watched as some of the Sken craft merged, before landing to pick up those who'd been marching.

"Guess that one's answered," Singh muttered.

The armies craft rose from the ground and skimmed over the forests, gathering speed as they went. There was an occasionally spate of coughing as the Sken craft spat globs of black matter at a few caretakers who remained lurking amidst the trees. The spider-like machines stood no chance and the column didn't even pause as it engaged the stragglers. Then they approached another familiar rabbit hole and the Manta unloaded from the Sken vessels. The column reformed and poured down the tunnel to Arcadia.

When they exited Selena and the others were surprised to find the tent camp still there, even the patch of dirt by the blood trees where Braxis had incinerated the massive reptilian creature remained blackened and grass-free. They continued without stopping at the camp but finally took a pause a few hours later. All the races posted guards and Selena found herself watching the Manta, as their insect-like faces constantly scanned the forests. Selena had mixed feelings about them. They were a horrible sight but she was glad they were on her side. Each time she looked at them she fought the urge to slaughter as many of them as she could. Then she felt the soothing presence of shadow in her mind, letting her know it was all right, they were safe. She glanced at Singh, saying, "Are you okay? I know you were with Bryn when we counter invaded his home planet, Theta. It must have been hell, particularly when you guys found the remains of his parents and sister in the garden."

"I'm fine," he replied. "Of course I think about it, breaking into the compound afterwards and killing the alien prisoners wasn't the best plan in the world. But Bryn had lost it and I couldn't let him go on his own, that's what got us sentenced to penal servitude. When you tried to get us pulled from the *Dutch Lady* mission it drove him nuts. It was me who suggested he come and talk to you about it. He just wanted to kill every one of them he could. It's kind of strange standing here besides them now, allies about to attack the ForeRunners. God knows what he would have thought about all this."

Selena had eventually come to love Bryn and God she wished he was here now. She knelt down and stroked Shadow, seeking comfort in his companionship.

They continued onwards shortly, and at midday entered a set of rabbit holes they'd not come across before. It was then Selena picked up a sudden warning from Shadow as they neared the exit of the smooth, white slopping tunnels. Ahead of them the Manta and Sken soldiers spilled from the alien craft and stormed through the exit.

"Prepare," Selena ordered over the battle net.

Even as she spoke the sound of fighting erupted from ahead. There were shouts and screams of pain, the high-pitched shriek and low hum of beam weapons and the crump of projectiles exploding. Then Selena and the others were out of the tunnels and into a world with an orange sky in which several moons of varying sizes roamed. Ahead of them stood an astonishingly tall silver city on a reddish sandy plain, beyond which lay a mirror-like ocean the colour of burnished gold. The city sparkled like a gem in the sunlight. Tall, needle-slim buildings stretched towards the heavens and between them ran lace-like gantries. Small craft, made bird-like by the distance, could be seen flitting between the buildings but as the army spread out a cloud of machines swept upwards from the city and raced towards them.

"That can't be good," Singh growled. "I've not seen anything like those before."

"I don't think any of us have," Selena replied, before adding over the battle net. "Standby, we've got incoming."

A multitude of weapons jutted from the enemy's half-moon shaped white craft and as they neared the vessels opened fire. For the first time Manta, Sken and human fought side by side. The ForeRunner beams slashed through their ranks and explosions flung bloodied and torn members of each race in all directions. Others simply burst into flame, screaming before dissolving into ash besides them. In return the Corps and Manta weapons hammered into the incoming ships and every hit the Sken made was a kill. Before long the combined assault began to take its toll on the ForeRunners.

More of the Sken ships began to come together and merge while other of their craft dropped from the heavens and joined the battle. As even more ships merged and the globes swelled they began to fire larger and larger rounds up into the heavens at unseen targets, and at the mass of incoming craft. The black rounds smothered the enemy vessels and ate into their hulls. As the gelatinous material hit the enemy craft they staggered, before dropping like stones.

"Spread out, lay down a suppressing fire," Selena ordered and the skimmers raced to distance themselves from each other, making them harder to hit. The soldiers fired from the sides of the skimmers, creating chaos amongst the enemy ships.

"Keep shooting," she ordered, then cursed as she saw the carpet of caretakers rushing towards them over the rosy sand like a plague of spiders.

As her men complied, the Sken changed tactics. Even while their vessels continued to merge countless thousands of Sken spilled out of the ships and joined their comrades in battle. Above them their craft bulged and fired huge blobs of goo at the city. As the buildings were splattered with the viscous liquid, it ran slowly down the walls like glutinous porridge, before turning into black dust and drifting away. The buildings were left with gaping holes, and many collapsed into the streets.

Shells exploded overhead, raining some kind of acid onto the Sken craft and the soldiers beneath them. The vessels trembled as though alive and uttered horribly deafening screeches as they themselves melted away. Unimaginable screams came from the infantry caught in the fiery downfall. Selena tore her eyes away as she saw her troops on the skimmers rip at their clothing even as they too dissolved. Others popped and crackled as they burst into flame. It was a scene Selena knew would haunt her forever, but the mega city was doomed. Those once proud towers were tumbling into the streets with loud, thunderous crashes while countless fires were fanned by the dry gentle wind that bore the multi-coloured smoke over the ocean.

"Gravpacks!" Selena bellowed and seconds later the humans leapt over the sides of the skimmers and floated towards the city like seeds on a stiff breeze. She breathed a sigh of relief when, a short while later, the power beams swatted many of the skimmers from the skies. Concerned for the safety of her men she ordered them to drop to the ground, where they ran alongside the Manta. The search teams released their lenars and they too bounded joyfully towards the enemy city, weaving in and out of the humans and aliens as they did so. The allied army washed over the torn and smoking city like a wave; ripping into screaming ForeRunner figures and leaving their bodies behind them.

Smoke, dust, the smell of blood and death was everywhere. There were enemy bodies in the street. Some still grasped weapons, although most looked like civilians caught up in the bloodshed. Selena was thankfully there were no children. Everywhere she looked bodies seemed to be around the same age, between thirty and forty. Even so, she felt sickened at the slaughter and then Shadow grabbed her attention.

"This way," she said to Singh, Braxis and four others. Shadow led the way down a small side street and they hurried after him, weapons ready. Kes and Roberts continued onwards without them, disappearing into the burning rubble that had once been a jewel of a city.

The doorway Shadow led them towards was filled with rubble and, shouting at everyone to get back Selena fired a grenade at a clear portion of wall next to it, ducking as chunks of the building flew in all directions. A darkened hole appeared through the clouds of dust and, surging forwards, they found themselves inside the building.

A rail-less flight of silver-coloured stairs led upwards to other floors. A group of panicking people in bright, multi-coloured clothes with weapons in their hands rushed down it towards them. They stopped when they saw Selena and the others, then screamed and danced insanely as the assault rifle in her arms juddered. The bullets slammed into them, casting their bodies from the stairs like confetti. They hit the floor with sickening slaps and lay still, blood splashing over the white tiles shot with veins of gold, and now bright arterial red. The Penal Corps moved forwards, slowly, carefully, their eyes and weapons covering every angle. As they passed the bodies one of them moved slightly and, without pausing, Shadow moved his head to one side, his teeth slicing through the woman's throat as if it were paper.

With a rumble masonry collapsed all around them and they ran towards a tall lime-green open archway beckoning from behind where the stairs kissed the floor. There they found a woman lying in a pile of debris, covered in white dust and a pistol of some kind in her hand. As the stunned-looking woman spotted them she managed to raise her weapon, but Selena fired a single shot from her assault rifle and watched as the woman's hand simply exploded. Selena smiled coldly as the woman screamed and clutched the ruined limb to her chest with her good hand. Selena walked forward slowly until she stood over her, the barrel of the assault rifle pointing down at the woman's eyes. Then she moved the barrel away and said, "Braxis, get her to a skimmer and then back to Loreen. I'm sure she'll come in handy."

Leaving Braxis and the others to it, Singh and Selena exited the building with Shadow besides them and stared up at the smoke-filled heavens. Far overhead lace-like white contrails wove through the orange sky. Here and there popcorn-shaped puffs of brilliant light blossomed silently then quickly faded, as ships further out in the system engaged and died. Closer by others exploded noisily, trails of smoke following them down to the ground where they tore into the city, the desert surrounding it or the motionless sea.

They could still hear the occasional rattle of guns, the whine and hiss of power beams, explosions and shrieks of agony. Using the battle net Selena asked her senior officers for a situation report and realised the battle was almost over. A short while later silence fell over the ruined city. Troops from the combined army appeared out of the ruins and began to walk through the streets. Occasionally there was a rapid burst of firing and then nothing, as small pockets of resistance were overcome. Selena's eyes were drawn back to the tangerine heavens, where puffs of light blazed for a moment or two as the battle in space raged on.

"The Sken took out some of the ForeRunners' orbital platforms as they exited the tunnel," Singh informed her. "Eliminating the ground defences and attacking the city allowed the Sken ships in the system to join the assault. Their losses would have been horrendous otherwise."

"Do you know if there are any of our vessels with them?" Selena asked.

"I doubt it. The impression I got was this world's too far away for either the Manta or ourselves. Our only road here is through those rabbit holes but the Sken ships are far more advanced, so the distance isn't a problem for them."

As Braxis and the female prisoner, whose stump of a hand was now bound, joined them in the street. They quickly took cover as there was a brain numbing rumble and a huge part of the metallic building opposite collapsed into the road, shrapnel flying in all directions.

"Interesting building material," Singh observed, as they climbed to their feet from behind a wall-like structure. "At this rate I can't see there being many survivors."

"Hopefully not," Selena replied. "But then we both know what the Manta are like, they won't stop the slaughter until one side or the other is finished."

"I still wish we'd killed them all with the *Dutch Lady*," Singh stated bitterly. "I don't trust those bugs as far as I can throw them, and given their size that's not very far."

Kes's voice came over the battle-net. "Captain, we'll be with you in a minute or two. Oh, and we have someone with us you'll be delighted to see. We're tracking you and have some friends with us." True to his world Philips and Roberts appeared in a skimmer a short while later, along with several fluttering Sken, the gigantic Skar...and Arthur.

"Well well…" Selena purred. "Hello, Arthur, though I shouldn't really call you that. He was a good and honest man, someone with integrity. I was kind of hoping we'd catch up with you sooner or later." Then she punched him straight in the face and knocked him to the floor. "Shutting down Capulet's defence systems cost us a lot of lives. You ran away once, I'm not going to let that happen again."

Selena watched him whiten as she stood over him and pointed her rifle at his right knee.

"Wait," he gasped. "Don't…"

Selena smiled coldly as she blew his leg off below the knee. "Never mind," she said, as his screams ripped at their ears. "I'm sure your medical expertise will allow you to grow another. Singh, put a battle dressing on that. If he still tries to crawl away then shoot his other goddamn leg off. Braxis, once he's patched up take this heap of shit with you as well. I'm sure Admiral Van Pluy would like to have a little chat with him. There are some questions that need answering, such as how he got away; and I want to see if he can help with the lenars."

Selena turned to the Manta, knowing it could understand her. "Do you mind if I ask where you received that head wound?"

That orange, glowing ball appeared over Skar's right shoulder and in an eldritch voice replied, "In the forests of Loreen. If anyone would know that, you would. I tracked the projectile."

"I thought so," she replied brightly. "Yes, you're right. It was me who gave you that wound. You were trying to escape by entering one of the Sken craft at the time with a chrysalis, if I recall correctly."

There was silence for a while and then the ball swirled. "That's correct, but would you have shot at a human carrying a sleeping child?"

Selena didn't know what to say for a moment, then blurted, "Your race attacked us, remember, not the other way around! You killed billions of our people, including the old, sick and infirm not to mention women and children. Then you have the gall to ask me that? Don't you dare, ever!" she fumed, her hands tightening around the assault rifle. "I wanted to be straight with you and, to be honest, ask you a favour. Perhaps, after that comment, now isn't a good time."

The orange ball swirled as Skar faced her squarely, looking down at her. "What favour?"

Selena tried to calm down. "The lenars are dying," she replied. "They were infected by a disease given to them by the ForeRunners, those you call the Cetra. As you were the architects of the original disease, my intention was to ask if you could help them."

The orange orb stopped swirling for a moment. "You care about these people?"

"Of course I bloody care," she spat. "They've done nothing wrong and just got caught up in your war, just as we did. Yes, so we fought them once before but that was a complete misunderstanding. The important thing now is there aren't many of the lenars left and, to be honest, their race doesn't deserve to go out like this."

"Then you are indeed different from the ancient ones," Skar said, rising up and down on his legs in a rhythmic motion, as if irritated. "They would have rejoiced in the lenars demise. So yes, we will help as much as we can, though that may not be much at all. There are so many variables. Your ForeRunners created this particular disease, not us. However, some of our people will need to be on Capulet if we are to help you."

"Agreed," Selena replied, a feeling of relief rushing through her. "Let me know what you need, and by the way we have one of the ForeRunners as a prisoner."

"We kill any of the Cetra on sight, so if you need it alive keep it away from us. We will also need access to the creatures."

"If you mean the lenars," Selena snapped. "Then we can transport you, or you can use your own ship to get to Capulet, but I'll need to know the details and arrange everything in advance or the vessel will be destroyed. As you can imagine, our people are a little touchy about your race at the moment. Once you are there your people can work with one of our scientists by the name of Cox, in the hope that between us we can find a cure. Oh, one more thing. The Cetra told us that sooner or later you would have used the weapons that devastated them against us as well. I need to know if that's true."

"No. We only used it against them once and that was because we had no choice. We would not do such a thing again."

"We need to leave, now," one of the Sken interrupted, the urgency of the thoughts pouring through their minds.

"What's the hurry?" Selena replied, with a frown.

"This place will be gone soon," came the reply.

Selena caught the feeling of unrest from Shadow and acted immediately. "Move out people," She ordered over the battle-net. "Get out of the city and back to the skimmers, something's coming and I've a feeling we don't want to be here when it arrives."

She watched as the Manta and lenars raced through the streets and out onto the ruddy plains beyond the city limits. As the skimmers filled up they flittered away. The Manta continued to lope along below them, while the Sken and remaining humans rose into the sky on their gravpacks and jetted away to safety.

"Officers, account for your men. I need to know how many we're down."

Landing at what they were told was a safe distance Selena and the others turned back to face the ruined city and saw hundreds of Sken ships swirling in clouds overhead. They flowed into one massive twisting multi-coloured blob and a huge black jellied mass detached and dropped towards the city, engulfing it. Moments later the black dust blew away, drifting over the sand dunes. Stunned she saw that most of the city had vanished. Then a second and third jellied mass fell, covering what little remained. Behind them the woman prisoner screamed and screamed, before reducing her cries to heart wrenching sobs.

"I'd save those tears if I were you," Selena told her. "I've a feeling you'll be shedding a lot more of them soon."

Chapter Fourteen

"What about any other bases on this world?" Selena asked, as she looked at the Sken. "There must have been far more than one."

"There were no other bases," came the reply. "Once the city was gone we destroyed their remaining weapon emplacements and production facilities. We can go now."

"What was so special about this planet?"

"It's from here they launched their attack on Loreen." The thoughts were like a wind blowing through the corridors of Selena's mind. "We've removed the threat."

"Well, surely they'll have other facilities elsewhere?"

The Sken said nothing but returned to their ships and entered the rabbit holes once more, followed by their ground troops and the marching Manta. In no time at all only humans remained on the alien world, listening to the red sand rustling over the dunes.

"Thank God they're on our side," Kes said, from besides Selena. "There's not a lot we could do against that weapon if they decided to use it against us."

"Precisely the point, isn't it," Selena replied. "We need to work out a defence, and quickly. You never know what's around the corner. Come on, let's get out of here. This place gives me the creeps."

The line of skimmers and soldiers who'd lost their transports re-entered the rabbit hole, and left the now desolate planet behind them.

*****

On returning to Loreen Selena ensured the two prisoners were safely locked up and then went to brief the Admiral.

Van Pluy was rapturous at first but stunned when she told him about how the Sken destroyed the city. He shared her concern. "I don't know how we're going to combat a weapon like that," he said. "Thankfully they're our allies, at least for the time being."

"Those are my sentiments exactly, Sir."

"Hmm…oh, Dillon I meant to tell you, a message came in from Capulet. Apparently your Aunt's back."

"Aunt May?"

"That's right. One of her neighbours contacted us. Apparently your aunt fled for her life after you got busted, but it looks like she's finally decided to return. You have some leave owing, so why don't you go see her and say your hellos? You should be able to hitch a ride from one of the traders at the spaceport, just check with the docking agents. They leave for Capulet all the time. Go ahead, you're dismissed Dillon. But be back in two weeks."

*****

Shadow travelled with Selena but left her once they touched down on Capulet. He'd decided to return to the forest, to frolic with friends and family, and no doubt update them on what had been happening.

As Selena walked up the road towards her aunt's house she felt a moment's trepidation. The last time she'd seen her aunt was before being sentenced for attempted murder. She paused for a moment to gather herself then, swallowing, knocked and waited. A few moments later the door opened and there she was.

Aunt May froze when she saw her, before rushing forward and wrapping her arms around Selena's shoulders. "What are you doing here? I heard all about what you've been up to. People are so proud. Fancy you turning out to be a hero, and then there's all this with the lenars. Oh my, when your mother and I were children they used to frighten us with stories about them."

"I expect the young lenars' heard pretty awful tales about us too," Selena replied, offering a silly grin. "But it's okay now. These days they'll only hurt you if you annoy them."

May rolled her eyes and planted a kiss on her cheek. "In any case, you'd better come in,"

"So, are you pleased to see me?" Selena asked, walking into the hall. She relished the comforting smell of cooking, spices and the floral freshener favoured by her aunt. The two-bedroom bungalow wasn't large and the burnished wooden flooring in the dining room still bore the same green hand-woven rugs she remembered so well from her youth. Aunt May's hair was now pure white and she'd put on so much weight her face seemed somehow cherubic. May was much smaller than Selena remembered, but how those family blue eyes still sparkled.

"Of course I'm pleased to see you, daft girl. I was surprised at the sentence they gave you, I'd expected execution. I know the others refused the offer and were killed. A lot of us left when they did that, and the riots kicked off, we were scared for our lives. When I heard the Manta had invaded I wondered if they'd let you back here to fight. I hear you met my gardener, she sent me a message to say you'd returned."

They entered the kitchen. It looked the same. The four old battle-scarred plain-wooden chairs with a matching but white-scrubbed dining table remained surrounded by household appliances and white-plasteel cupboards. Everything was in the same place it always had been. Selena glanced at the antique dust-covered hunting rifle that lay in brackets across one wall, then pulled out a chair and sat at the dining table watching her aunt make locally-grown Jasmine tea. The warm, welcoming smell of baking bread filled the kitchen. It took Selena back to her childhood, but the clink of cups on the table brought her swiftly to her senses.

"You know why I'm here, don't you?" Selena asked at last.

"I imagine it's not to ask how I am, despite the fact I brought you up after your mother died. Maybe you've come to ask why I didn't attend the court case, when you were convicted of those awful crimes."

"No, that's not the reason," Selena replied softly, "although I'd be interested to know why you weren't there during the trial. We're family. In fact you're all I have left so naturally I was really disappointed you didn't come to support me."

"I would have," May replied sadly, "but I couldn't bear to see you sentenced to death, let alone taken out and killed. You've changed, Selena, I've followed your progress and been shocked at the things you've done. Look at you. Your eyes are like chips of pure ice, devoid of all warmth. What happened to the lovely young slip of a girl I once knew, the one who used to bring me a cup of tea every morning and help me with chores around the house?"

"She died a very long time ago, around the same time my parents did."

May's bottom lip quivered for a moment. She took a deep breath. "Okay, let's start there, shall we? I was devastated when your mother killed herself, though she knew I loved you like my own daughter and would always care for you. It's pointless dwelling on such things, what's done is done.

"You know that I never married or had children of my own. So, can you even imagine how I felt when I had to watch how those so-called friends of yours twist and pervert you, imagining themselves revolutionaries to justify their evil plots? They dug away at you, Selena, filling your mind with ridiculous ideas until all you could think about was revenge and death. You should have been enjoying your childhood, but instead you were focused on murder. I knew what you were up to and tried to talk you out of it, as I'm sure you recall."

"Yes, I remember."

"Selena, I told you time and again revenge never solves anything. It only gets more people killed. But you joined that gang of mongrels anyway, and yes I know what you're going to say, they were your friends, but to me they were nothing less than a band of murdering scum. There's was never any proof the Queens guard did anything wrong, despite what people claimed. Yet you killed them without a seconds thought. Oh Selena, I didn't want to lose you as well as your parents. This works both ways. You're the only family I have left too. Let's face it, I did lose you and then had to run for my life. I'm sorry to say this, but I expected so much better from you."

"You're straight to the point, as always, Aunt May. So, we disappointed each other," Selena replied, leaning back and balancing her wooden chair on two legs.

May's lips thinned. "Don't get smart with me, my girl. I knew your mother was up to something but not exactly what. I thought it would be some kind of demonstration. I was worried she'd end up in gaol and tried to talk her out of it. I kept telling her if she went to prison it would be unfair on you. It's not that I don't love you, because I do, but a girl needs her own mother's love and upbringing."

"She didn't listen to you though, did she?" Selena leant forward so that the front wooden chair legs hit the floor with a loud clack, her eyes intent. "Maybe you should have tried a little bit harder."

There was a loud ping from the far side of the kitchen, indicating that the bread was ready. Aunt May stood and walked over to the sideboard and, removing the contents from the pan, left the bread to cool on a wire tray. Then she returned to her seat and poured the tea, placing a small white cup of the fragrant deep-green brew in front of Selena. She watched her niece carefully over the rim of her cup while blowing on the steaming liquid and finally taking a sip. "No she didn't listen, which is where you get it from my girl. She was too twisted by grief."

Selena was quiet for a moment, and rocked back and forth. "I met the Queen again recently. We had quite an interesting chat."

May's eyes narrowed. "Ah, so that's why you're here. I'm surprised you left her alive. That fiery temper of yours is something else you get from your mother." Lowering her cup, she looked down into the green depths in which a few loose leaves lurked. "You've questions to ask?"

"The Queen told me you all used to be close friends. Is it true?"

"Yes."

"So tell me about it."

May's gaze flicked straight to Selena, and then she took a deep breath and composed herself. "We all knew each other when we were children. After all, this city isn't such a big place. We even attended the same school together. Your father and Miranda were childhood sweethearts, before she became Queen and, as per tradition, lost all her names."

"You're lying..."

"No, Selena, I'm not. Why would I? You're all I have left and I have no reason to do so. You need to know the truth."

Finally Selena dropped her gaze. She knew May was telling the truth. She could tell by her look, gesture, her tone of voice and the underlying sadness that told of complete honesty.

"I still find our adherence to those old protocols ridiculous," her aunt continued, "for royalty to simply become known as 'the King' or 'the Queen'. I expect you know from your school history lessons this tradition dates back to our colonisation, when our rulers were the only royalty on this world. Unlike Earth, who had so many

Kings and Queens ruling various countries it was no wonder they got confused. Each of those needed a name to follow their title, so people could figure out who they were talking about.

"Our Monarchs decided early on that because they were the only rulers on this world then their titles would serve as their name; until they eventually died of course, and they got their old names back. It's a timeless constant that marks us apart from other worlds, Earth in particular."

Selena picked up the small, delicate cup and blew at the steam before taking a sip. "Well, Earth's practically a wasteland now but you're changing the subject."

Aunt May huffed. "Very well...Miranda and Raynor were very close from an early age and eventually became lovers. That's right," she said, forestalling Selena by holding up a pale liver-spotted hand in which thick blue veins stood out. "You may not like it but they were together a long time, long before your mother. Then one day the King saw Miranda and claimed her for his own, as is their want. God knows what he saw in her, or what your father did either come to that. Miranda once had a nice personality and there was something about her that drew people to her, but only the blind could have thought she was attractive.

"Of course your father was devastated. One moment Miranda was there with him and the next she was gone. There was no warning, no saying of goodbyes. Everyone knew what had happened, naturally. Let's face it, the royalty and their minions have been doing this sort of thing since the foundation. Her disappearance bore the hallmark of the nobility and so all her family could do was pray they'd eventually let her go.

"Some time later Miranda's parents received a letter, telling them she was the 'King's guest' for a while." May snorted. "Such things never change. If the victims are lucky they might be eventually released, but many disappear forever. As do any relatives or friends who create waves."

"I know all this," Selena growled, "but what I don't understand why the people haven't stood up for themselves, apart from when they rebelled after Ma died."

There was a silence for a moment and Selena glanced around. The white-framed reflective windows were still there, although they looked somewhat old and tired now. Those surprisingly strong panes darkened or lightened depending on the sunlight and you could only see outwards. The combination of both was a strong defence against the lenars, who'd often leapt through the glass windows of early settlements.

"They have paid informants everywhere. They'll report you for the smallest transgression and be well paid for it: although many did so to gain favour because they were afraid for their families," Aunt May said bitterly. "Look at what happened when your mother was killed. Thousands died in the uprising. Our royalty have never understood compassion or mercy, only killing and self-interest."

May got up and walked over to the fridge, fussing about with her back turned to Selena, who waited patiently for her to gather her thoughts and continue. When May faced her again it was with two plates of golden-crusted apple pie and thick yellow fresh cream.

"I expect you're hungry, dig in. You used to love this as a child. It's a very old family recipe. We add nutmeg to the apple," she added with a conspiratorial wink, "and that spice is very hard to come by in these trying times."

"Do you mind carrying on with the story?" Selena asked. She picked up the spoon from the red rose decorated plate and took a spoonful of pure heaven.

May huffed again. "Your mother always liked Raynor, and it was only natural she tried to comfort him when Miranda disappeared. But, as the months passed, things changed. Her love for your father was obvious to anyone who looked, and gradually he fell for her too. Within a few years they were married. Naturally Miranda found out and was furious, as you can imagine. I think when people become royalty they take their brain out and put a stupidity chip in, because when the King died all hell broke loose."

"In what way?"

"Eat your pie and drink your tea, Selena, there's more in the pot. Let me tell the tale in my own time."

Doing as she was bid Selena relished the sweetness of the desert, the bitterness of the tea and the many memories the two bought back. She used to sit in this chair as a girl, swinging her legs back and forth while she did her homework, because her feet didn't reach down to the copper-toned tiles.

"Miranda's spies told her all about your parents of course, but there was nothing she could do about it while the King was alive. As is tradition she inherited the throne when he passed away. He hadn't been dead very long when she began to take a string of lovers, one after another, acting as if she didn't care." May laughed and wiped a tear from her eye. "She was desperate for a child and of course needed an heir, but not one of those poor souls made her pregnant. Finding out about you only added fuel to the fire. Then a hand-delivered summons arrived at your parents' home, demanding your father attend the Queen. He declined of course and wrote her a reply, giving it to the liverymen to take back."

"So what happened?" Selena asked, intrigued.

"They came for him that very night. Your mother tried to stop them but was beaten black and blue. I visited her in the hospital. Shortly afterwards your parents were divorced by royal decree and, of course, they had no say in the matter. Queen Miranda then forced your father to marry her and your mother never saw him alive again, although she did receive a few smuggled letters."

"I was told the Queen had him killed," Selena said, watching her aunt closely.

"Actually we were told he took his own life, and that was from a number of sources but your mother refused to believe it. She was convinced the Queen had him murdered because in his letters Raynor said he'd refused to pleasure her, and more than anything the Queen wanted a child by him. Selena, this may be hard for you to understand but I know how much Miranda loved your father and I'm convinced she didn't have him murdered. She cared far too much for him, do you see? I believe your father killed himself, because he knew Miranda was besotted and would never let him go."

Selena jumped to her feet and slammed her cup onto the table, the dark-green contents spilling onto the brown wooden surface as the handle came off in her hand. "That's rubbish and you know it!"

"Actually it's true, so calm down and take a seat." When Selena did so, her aunt continued. "When your mother found out about Raynor's death she was inconsolable." May paused for a moment or two, and then added, "It's ironic really, because I always thought your mother would end up with Miranda's older brother, he thought the world of her."

"I didn't know the Queen had a brother."

"Oh yes, Simon was a good man but when the King kidnapped Miranda, Simon got in trouble for speaking out against him. Then a 'plot' was discovered about Simon intending to rescue her. All utter nonsense of course, it was just a way to get rid of him. He was sentenced to the Penal Regiments, just as you were. There was a recruitment surge then, too."

"Really? Why?" Selena asked with a puzzled frown.

"The old colonies were filled to bursting and they needed troops to protect the new ones and to stop rebellions. It's been the same throughout history, as colonies expand and grow stronger they want to split off and go out on their own. Of course the Federation of Man couldn't afford to let that happen. Consequently there was lots of danger and the Regular Forces, often made up of gentry who bought rank, didn't want to take the risks, so they drafted in the criminals and miscreants as a form of restorative justice for their crimes. Their valuables were confiscated and given to their victims or their families, and the consequent military service was viewed as payback to the community of mankind as a whole. It saves the expense of gaols and they're given the option of working in the mines instead."

"The mines are just legalised slavery," Selena snorted, "and a death sentence in itself. So Simon got arrested and sentenced for trying to save his sister?"

"That's right, and he was your father's best friend. Like I said, we all played together as children."

"Simon and Miranda: ha, they even sound like royalty. So what was their family name?"

Aunt May took a sip of her tea and sat back in her chair. "Van Pluy. Apparently he's an Admiral now."

Selena's breath froze. For once she was unable to utter a word.

"Are you all right, girl?"

"I…"

"Selena?"

"Sorry, but I need to go."

May stared at her for a moment. "I'm not sure what's wrong but there's something you need to take into account."

"Really, what might that be?"

May put down her cup; her eyes boring intently into Selena's. "For heaven's sake, you're not listening at all are you? I just told you Queen Miranda married your father, which means he became King. If you can get your head around that then you'll realise it makes Miranda your stepmother. What's more, because the Queen never had any children of her own it means you're next in line to the throne, and I'm pretty sure she's not fond of the idea at all."

Selena chest felt tight and she grabbed the table to stop herself falling. "I'm going to wake up in a moment and find all of this is a nightmare. Like I said, I need to go. There's lot I have to think about."

"Yes, I've no doubt there is. Well, do come back when you're all done and we'll chat some more. Perhaps next time you could stay for some dinner?"

"Yeah, thanks, that would be nice." For the first time since she was a child Selena hugged her aunt and kissed her lightly on the cheek, marring the white make-up she'd not noticed before. May smiled and that twinkle glinted in her eye once more. "Ah, there you are, my girl. I thought I'd lost you."

"See you soon, Aunt May. I'll think about what you said, but I want you to know it doesn't make the slightest bit of difference. The Queen is directly responsible for the death of my parents and sooner or later she's going to pay for it. The fact she's my stepmother won't come into it at all."

"Well you take care, child."

Selena left May sipping her tea and shut the door behind her, thoughts in turmoil. Van Pluy had to know who she was. The big question was, had he taken her under his wing for the sake of her father's friendship, or because the Queen wanted him to keep an eye on her? If she was indeed next in line for the throne then it was an opportunity to bring law and order to Capulet. That, and the thirst for revenge, was more than enough reason for her to do what she longed to.

Walking down the lane back towards the city proper, Selena's lips curled into a smile and she gave a half laugh. Then she froze in mid step, the hair on the back of her neck stood straight up. Something was wrong and she knew it. She eyed the waist high grass on either side of the dirt road. That's where she'd be, if she was them. Knowing there was no chance of making it Selena tried anyway. She dived to her left, rolled and dived again.

That's when they shot her.

The stun beam took her in the midst of the second roll, swatting aside her like an insect. The pain was unbearable and she laid quivering and jerking in the dirt, hand close to her side arm but unable to pull it. Blood flowed down her face where she'd landed and taken the skin off. Selena had made it far too easy for them. She'd become complacent more fool her, and now she'd pay the consequences.

Laying there unable to move she watched as ten men in the uniform of the royal guard rose out of the grass and sauntered towards her, taking their time. Four of them picked her up and threw her into the back of a skimmer that appeared out of nowhere. The next thing Selena knew she was waking up in what felt like a ship's darkened hold. She was still in her uniform but chained to a metal bulkhead. A door opened, light filtered in and to her dismay the Queen strode in, the smile on her face saying it all.

"Hello again, Selena," she purred. "I have to say I'm sorry to find you like this. I'd so hoped we could become friends, but when you threatened me in front of my staff…well I couldn't let it slide, now could I? Having said that, I did at least wait until the emergency was over.

"The fact you saved Capulet means I won't have you killed, step daughter. But, rest assured, if you ever return to this world you and your kin will be executed immediately. Your threats on my life were made long after the pardon given to the Penal Corps, which means those crimes are punishable."

The Queen squatted down in her all-in-one silver trouser outfit, with a black pistol belt at her waist. She grasped Selena's face with one hand, squeezing her cheeks between fingers and thumb. The agony as the Queen dug her fingers into the ripped and torn flesh focused Selena, and she relished the feeling of the fresh blood pouring down her face.

"Despite the fact you once tried to kill me you're the last link I have to Raynor, and I really do care for you. Many of the inner royal-circle wanted you dead a long time ago, but I saved you from the death penalty. It was me who spoke to the off-world judge all those years ago and suggested the penal squads as an alternative. How could I possibly have you killed? You look so much like him."

Queen Miranda's gaze was one of icy triumph, as she tore her hands away and stood, wiping the blood away down the side of her trousers, staining them. "I came to realise I was wrong in trying to reclaim your father all those years ago. I was too late. He'd already fallen in love with your mother by then. He took his own life and I can't forgive myself for that. But no matter what you believe, I didn't kill him.

"Here's something else for you to consider. Your Aunt May left this world once because she thought I'd have her assassinated. I could have quite easily, of course. I knew exactly where she was but I left her alone. To catch a rat you need a piece of cheese, and she was my key to you. I knew if you came back she'd return too, all I had to do was get a message to her. That's right, the friend who told your aunt you were here was one of my people. May won't escape me a second time. She will be watched very closely from now on, and that means you'll do exactly as I say."

Miranda's smile was cold and chilling. "So, dear step daughter, bear in mind that if anything at all happens to me then the assassins I've paid will know exactly where to find your aunt, and will follow the instructions I've left for them."

"What do you get out of this?" Selena asked. "Why not just kill me and be done with it?"

"Because your father made me promise that I'd never hurt you. Whatever else you think of me I loved your father and he knew I'd never break my word to him."

Selena spat at her as the blood continued to drip from the side of her face. Then came the cold touch of metal against her cheek and she heard the hiss of compressed gas. As she collapsed the chains kept her face from hitting the floor, and her arms above her head.

*****

A few hours after she awoke Selena was dragged out of the ship and into the spaceport on Loreen. Thrown into the back of a skimmer she was transported a short distance before being dragged straight to the corridor outside of Van Pluy's office, where she was made to stand and wait. When Selena was finally marched in he was sat at a long table on the right of two other senior officers, Admiral Anderson and someone in the middle that she didn't know. The sergeant-at-arms kept her at attention.

"The Queen of Capulet testifies," Anderson began, "that in front of witnesses you threatened to cut off her eyelids and kill her. We have affidavits from those same witnesses here, in addition to additional evidence. What do you have to say in your defence, Captain?"

Selena kept silent, knowing for her to speak would do no good at all. Then they played the recordings of her threatening the Queen over Van Pluy's wall screen followed by the sworn testimonials of her guards. She should have seen that coming. It had been stupid of her to forget that the royal chambers and passageways were monitored by cams. Selena avoided Van Pluy's eyes as the officer in the middle spoke again.

"Captain Dillon, the court finds you are guilty of the charges against you. Your promotion to captain was subject to trial and approval, therefore you're reduced to the rank of commander with immediate effect. You're also sentenced to five year's additional servitude along with ten lashes. Take her away."

Two soldiers dragged her out into the morning sun. The entire garrison had been mustered and stood to attention in long silent black silent ranks. They chained her wrists and ankles to the metal frame and stripped her to the skin, as she knew they would. All of them stared straight ahead, not one attempted eye contact or even a glimpse of her naked body. Then she saw Roberts look her way, and give a slow but perceptible nod. Besides her, Kes remained immobile.

The pain, when it came, was indescribable but Selena bit back her cries as the leather slashed through her tender skin. They loudly counted seven strikes across her naked back and buttocks, the last three across her bare breasts, stomach and thighs. Not once did she cry out. Selena was in a different place now, where she could shut herself away from the agony and disgrace. A place where Bryn, Samantha and so many dead friends held her hand, whispered in her ears, consoled her and told her there would be a day of reckoning.

When they finally threw the buckets of saline solution across her raw and bleeding wounds Selena almost passed out. Released from the chains she staggered, still naked to the sickbay. None of the soldiers standing to attention in the parade ground made a sound as she left.

The sickbay door creaked as it was held open for her and she walked silently, doubled up past the queue of soldiers and civilians waiting to register their complaints. Another held-open door led to where the doctors waited. None of them spoke as they sprayed her wounds with anaesthetic before laying her down on a gurney. There was a sharp hiss of compressed gas and she knew they would heal her wounds and the cosmetic surgeons disguise the scars, making her look whole once again.

But even as she dropped off to sleep Selena smiled savagely and began to make plans once more.

Acknowledgements

My special thanks go to the following for their feedback
and input:
Jason Kurt Easter – Beta Reader
Peter Wilhelmsen – Beta Reader
Robert Harkess – Beta Reader
Mark Rutley - Photographer

About the Author...

As a child Mark was bought up in Slough and used to read up to three paperbacks a day. At the age of 17 he joined the Royal Navy as a radio operator and says he's so lucky to have seen so much of the world. While always interested in writing he began to do so more seriously following his experiences during the Falklands War, in which he served aboard HMS Invincible. His short stories have been published in a wide variety of media and he has also written prolifically about the martial arts for magazines such as *Combat* and *Martial Arts Illustrated.*

Passing his MA in Professional Writing with Falmouth University he also holds Diplomas in Creative Writing, Copywriting and Proofreading. As well as working full time for Southampton University Mark works part time as a Copywriter, Author and Editor. His writing includes copy, features and fiction. While he writes in all genres his fiction is primarily SF, fantasy and horror.

Appearing in several anthologies, including *Auguries, Escape Velocity, Write to Fight* and *Monk Punk*, Marks first novel 'A Pride of Lions' hit number 1 in the kindle scifi/colonisation charts. This novel, *'The Cull of Lions',* is the second instalment in *The Darkening Stars* series.

Other Solstice titles you might enjoy…

A Pride of Lions

By: Mark Iles

When Selena Dillon is caught in an assassination attempt on her planet's ruler, she finds herself sentenced to twenty-five years servitude in the most feared military force, the Penal Regiments. Much to her surprise she enjoys the harsh military life and is quickly selected for officer training.

But something's wrong, worlds are falling silent. There's no cry for help and no warning, just a sudden eerie silence. When a flotilla of ships is despatched to investigate they exit hyperspace to find themselves facing a massive alien armada. Outnumbered and outgunned the flotilla fight a rearguard action, allowing one of their number to slip away and warn mankind.

As worlds fall in battle, and mankind's fleets are decimated, Selena is selected to lead a team of the Penal Regiment's most battle-hardened veterans, in a last ditch attempt to destroy the aliens' home world. If she fails mankind is doomed. Little does Selena know that one of her crew is a psychopathic killer and another is the husband of his victim.

Can she hold her team together, get them to their target and succeed in the attack? Selena knows that if she fails then there will be nothing at all left to go home to.

A Conniseur of the Bizarre
By: Mark Iles

A carful of police officers swerves in the rain to avoid a shadowy figure. Detective Chets Owen and his two companions immediately recognise the local lunatic, O'Neal, but they're shocked to see a gun in his hand. Then O'Neal mentions that he knows where a missing child is. Does he, or doesn't he, and is O'Neal really who he seems?

RobotPlanet: A Story For James W.
By: Helen Alexander

Boltolomew lives the peaceful life of a cleaning robot on the distant, long forgotten planet of Greta, until the day he finds an old music box in his garage. He doesn't know what it is, but he can't take his CPU off it for a moment. When he shows it to his friends, they're just as puzzled.

The mysterious box is just the beginning of Boltolomew's troubles: soon he begins seeing a Spaceship landing on his way home from work, although no one else can see it, and then even stranger things start happening. One night, visitors emerge from the craft, only to vanish into thin air, leaving Boltolomew confused and overheated from too much thinking. Boltolomew's friends become concerned for him, and his Supervisor at the Cleaning Factory, Chief Bot, decides to have him reprogrammed.

Boltolomew doesn't want to be reprogrammed, however, because it would make him forget the things he saw - well, he's pretty sure that he saw them, anyway. He must make a difficult choice: stay in the City without any memory of his previous self, or run away and face the dangers of the desolate Junk Yard. But most of all, Boltolomew wants to know: who are the visitors from the Spaceship, and why can't anyone else see it?

For more Solstice titles, visit our online store:
http://solsticepublishing.com/bookstore/